THE
KING
OF
CLUBS

a novel by
Howard Goldberg

THE KING OF CLUBS

by

Howard Goldberg

PARTHENON PRESS
New York

PARTHENON PRESS

Manufactured in the United States of America

First Paperback Edition, 2011
ISBN 0-615437-71-0

First Hardcover Edition, 1982
ISBN 0-942276-01-9

Library of Congress Catalog No.: 81-85466
Goldberg, Howard
The King of Clubs
New York: Parthenon Press

to
jane r. kessler
(1950 - 1982)

Dear James,

Well, here we go again. For the hundreth time it looks like I've really stuck my foot in it. I just never seem to learn. Anyway, I have to somehow get my thoughts together, and a letter to you seems like the best way.

About three weeks ago I was in a bar on the upper west side and I met this guy named Bill. He was incredibly goodlooking and built like the proverbial brick shithouse. A hunk. We talked for quite some time and he bought me a drink. One thing led to another and we eventually wound up going back to his place and the rest I will leave to modesty and your imagination. Well, we really got along well and subsequently started seeing each other quite often and within five days I had moved in with him. Quite frankly I don't know why I chose to do that, but I guess at the time it seemed even practical as his apartment was closer to my office than my own. I didn't really think it would be permanent anyway.

He's a real gentleman and genuinely courteous. His concern over both myself and my life is touching and much appreciated. When I talk about the things that are bothering me I'm absolutely amazed by his concentration and attention. I can talk intelligently with him about all aspects of my work and never have the feeling that he is patronizing me. It often seems too good to be true. His life, however, is as closed to me as mine is open to him. He doesn't work. I have no idea what it is that he does. His apartment is beautiful, large, expensive and decorated to the hilt, yet I have

1

no idea whatsoever where his money comes from. He insists on paying for everything and refuses to hear of it when I try to pick up a tab. He spends money like it was going out of style. You know what he does? He works out. Every day he leaves for the gym and works out. He runs, he lifts weights, he trains. Not for anything in particular, he just trains.

In all the time that I've been with him up until now I haven't found one thing in his apartment that would give any indication as to his history (where he went to school, where he's from, etc.). He's a real mystery man. I guess his family probably has lots of money and he lives off that. But, the curious part is that he doesn't seem to have the attitude towards money that a guy from a rich background would have. He seems to enjoy spending his money the way a man who has earned it would.

He talks about death all the time. He always wants to know what I think happens after you die. Whether I want to live to be old. Stuff like that. He can get downright morbid. He's about 35 years old. Also, he has scars all over his body. What if he's crazy? I really don't know him all that well. I once knew a girl who was a self-mutilator. She used to slash herself with razor blades and smash her hands through glass doors. Neat stuff like that. Jesus, I hope he's not some kind of lunatic. Did you see "Looking for Mr. Goodbar"? Call my mother if you don't hear from me... I like roses. See what I mean about being morbid? Well anyway, I don't know what the point to all this is other than to

2

let you know about all the neat trash that can be picked up in New York. How are you? How's that guy you were seeing? Anything happening there? Keep in touch and I'll see you soon.

Love,
John

Bill Thomas was halfway across Sixth Avenue when the light turned yellow. He had to leap to avoid the cars which were, as is often the case with New York City traffic, grossly anticipating the light. He was carrying a gym bag and wearing a sweat suit. He entered a large, modern skyscraper through a small delivery port on a side street and took a private elevator to the top floor. As he passed through the reception area he nodded to some people that were lounging around. He went into the locker room. After talking to a couple of the men that he passed, he deposited his bag in his locker and went through to the gym. A tall, powerful looking man smacked him on the back.

"Hey, Bill, what's happening?" said the man. "You got anything up this week?"

"Hey, man, how you doing?" said Bill. "Nah, I'm free and clear."

"How lucky can you get."

"Yeah, well I've got Jones on Monday."

"No shit... that should be something!"

"Yeah..."

3

"Hey, good luck, man, I gotta be running." He smacked Bill on the back again.

"Yeah," said Bill. "Take it easy."

Bill crossed the room, found some free mat space and started to do his warm-up calisthenics. He stretched his muscles the way a dancer would. Slowly at first and then finally bending quite supply. He was finely proportioned and moved very gracefully. A middle-aged man in a sweat suit with close cropped grey hair came over and watched him go through his paces. He looked like he had probably once been a Marine.

"How you feeling, Bill?"

"Hey, Lou, okay. I feel fine... how you doing?"

"Me, I'm okay. You look pretty good."

"Oh yeah, Lou. I never felt better."

"That's great," said Lou. "Listen, I'd like to see you do about five miles today. You could do a little light weight work, too. Then I got this guy Scharf I want you to do some wrestling with."

"Okay, Lou, that sounds great."

"Yeah, why don't you meet us over in the small mat room about 3, okay."

"Sure thing, Lou."

Malcolm Anderson was in the tool and die business. He had been ever since his father had died and that was quite some time ago. Now, he was the chairman of the board and principal stockholder in a publicly owned business that grossed in excess of two billion dollars per year. He was very well off and always had been. He liked the power and prestige that went with his position. He also liked his family. He liked his home on the North Shore of Long Island and he liked the many things he was able to buy with his money. He had joined the Club in 1959 at the behest of his best friend Dick Alston. He and Alston had been at Harvard together and had known each other since they were children. Their families had both had summer homes in the Thousand Islands during the thirties. Dick had joined the Club two years prior to first approaching Malcolm. He told him at the time that it had taken over six months for the Board to screen him after his name had been submitted as a possible member. He paid the $200,000 bond and joined. In the twenty-one years that had passed since he had first taken the elevator to the top floor of the Northrop Tower he had yet to lose interest. His fascination with the Club was still as strong as it had been that first day.

Physically the Club was beautiful. It could well afford to be. Its membership roster was filled to overflow with the names of some of the wealthiest and most influential people in New York and, by extension, the world. Off the reception area were common rooms, dining areas and bedrooms. There were computer terminals and stock exchange readouts so that members could keep in touch with their work. The main auditorium had both floor level viewing and balcony seating. There were three hundred members. Depending on when they had joined, they had all posted a bond of between $200,000 and $1,000,000. Annual maintenance of their membership was also very high. Generally around $200,000 per year. They were all members for life.

After he had finished his workout for the day Bill hit the showers. He was glad he hadn't had to work too hard. Lou always planned it that way. Tomorrow would be much heavier and then he would have the weekend off. Monday, just warmups. Lou told him to take a rubdown and whirlpool before leaving. The rubdown he could handle but he hadn't much patience for whirlpools. They left him feeling flushed and sleepy, but he figured Lou knew best. He also had no intention of being fined. More for the emotional aggravation than for the financial blow that it represented. He hated having Lou on his tail. He almost dozed off in the hot water as he ran through his mind what he would tell John when he got back to his place. He was a really sweet guy, but it was time he left. He'd already allowed him to stay at least a week too long. He laughed to himself. Christ, Lou would have a fucking heart attack if he knew about this. All the way to the shores of Tripoli.

John was preparing dinner when he heard the key in the door. He was pretty excited as he had stopped by the half-price ticket stand on Broadway on his way home from work. He had gotten good seats to "A Chorus Line" for that evening and he was going to surprise Bill. Since the tickets were already in his pocket, paid for and ready to go, Bill could hardly object and he would at least be able to feel as if he were pulling a little bit of his own weight. Dinner was to set the mood.

"Hey, Bill... Hi!"

"Oh hi, John, how you doing?" He threw his bag across the room. It landed on the couch.

"Dynamite," he said as he crossed the kitchen to meet Bill at the door. He tried to give him a hug. The thought repulsed Bill. He realized he wasn't all that thrilled with John's presence any longer, so perhaps the time schedule had worked out just right after all.

"I missed you," said John as he turned back towards the kitchen. He sensed something was coming. It was hardly the first time. Bill went into the bedroom to change his clothes.

"How was your day?" asked John cautiously.

"I can't hear you," said Bill with a note of irritation in his voice. Jesus Christ, he thought, I can't believe the fucking guy is actually making dinner. Boy, this one has got to go. Well anyway, with a little luck he'd be down in the Bahamas next week scheming chicks and catching a little R and R. This part, though, was always sticky. He went into the living room and switched on the tube.

"What're you making?" he asked. He began switching the channels.

"A pot roast... I hope you like pot roast. It'll be ready in ten minutes."

"Yeah," Bill said, "I like pot roast. Hey, you got any beer in there?"

Malcolm Anderson reached for the black phone on his desk as it rang. It was his direct line and only a few people knew how to reach him on it.

"Anderson," he said.

"Malcolm? Dick."

"Hey, Dick... how are you?"

"Fine, fine. How about you?"

"No problems. Can't complain. Hey, where've you been keeping yourself?"

"Mostly behind this desk." He laughed.

"Haven't seen you over at the Club at all."

"I know. It's been absolutely insane over here. I haven't had a chance to do anything. In fact, that's one of the reasons I was calling. Murray told me Bill Thomas was up tonight."

"That's right."

"Are you going?"

"Wouldn't miss it." Malcolm smiled.

"Great! How about if I pick you up and we go over a little early and grab a bite?"

"Sounds good."

"Then I'll see you later."

"Fine." He started to put the receiver down and then brought it quickly back to his face.

"Hey, Dick!"

"Uh-huh?" He was still there.

"Listen. Could you make it about 5:30. I forgot I have a meeting that I'm going to have to cut short as it is."

"No problem."

Leon Jones was huge. He was sarcastically known as L'il Leon but the humor was, for the moment, lost on Bill Thomas. The blow that he had just ducked could have taken his head off. He wheeled around swiftly to his right and caught Leon with a kick in the stomach. As Jones bent over from the force of the kick, Bill tried to catch him from above with a punch on the neck. Leon caught it on his forearm. The auditorium was packed this Tuesday evening. Both Jones and Thomas were very popular. Jones mostly for his enormous bulk and Thomas mostly for his speed and style. It was pretty much even odds on the outcome although Bill was clearly the favorite. The auditorium, which was not very large, afforded perfect views and a precarious closeness for all save the balcony spectators. The room smelled of sweat. There was a roar as Jones caught Bill on the upper left arm drawing first blood. They were fighting with long knives and the double edged hunting knife that Leon was using had left a very deep wound where it had struck. Thomas was obviously stunned and with difficulty stopped a lunge for his midsection at the last second. It probably would have ended the contest. Bill, using the momentum of Leon's thrust against him, pulled the larger man through his central balance and stabbed him in the upper chest under his arm. He could feel the blade glance Leon's ribs. The bell rang.

"These guys are great," said Malcolm Anderson. He and a small group of men were sitting close to the matted section of the auditorium where the two men were fighting.

"Yeah," said Dick Alston, "do you remember that fight that Thomas had last year with Nowicki? Jesus I didn't think either one of them would walk away from that!"

"Hey, Dick," said a small, balding man to Alston's right. "You wanna press that bet or what?"

"You gonna give me odds, Murray? My man's pretty knocked up. He isn't going to be able to use that left arm at all I wouldn't think."

"They'll patch him up as good as new! What're you kidding? I'll give you 3 to 2 on any additional money you want to bet."

"Murray, we'll just make that two thousand more then... and you can just pay that directly to the bar man. Thanks for the drinks, buddy."

"Pretty sure of yourself, aren't you?" said Murray.

"Naw, I just slipped Jones a mickey, that's all."

The bell. Both men have had the wounds they received in the previous period dressed as best as possible. They are both favoring their left sides. As they approach each other in the center Bill Thomas feints with his knife and kicks Jones in his wounded area with his left. The pain is great and he starts slashing out wildly so that he can keep Thomas off him until he is able to regain his composure. Bill kicks him again. This time in the shins. Jones cuts him on the calf. It is only superficial however and Bill backs off immediately. As he turns around low to deliver a roundhouse kick he walks right into Jones's fist. It breaks his nose, while the blade of Jones's knife lays open his cheek. They are very close together at this point and Bill thrusts blindly. He stabs Jones cleanly through the heart as he himself collapses.

"Oh shit," says Murray, "I think Jones just bought the farm!"

The crowd is on its feet as a team of aides with stretchers runs onto the mats. Jones is dead. Thomas will live. Lou and a man with a doctor's bag are examining him as Jones's body is placed on a stretcher for removal.

"C'mon you guys," says Dick, "I'll buy you all a drink. It looks like I'm the big winner tonight." He pokes Murray playfully in the ribs. Murray is not particularly amused.

"Ow! That stings like hell!"

"C'mon, Bill, calm down," said Lou Geller, using all his strength to hold the overwrought fighter in place. "The doc's got enough problems without having to worry about you. Right, Doc?"

"Sure, Lou." The doctor reached into his bag for a sterile suture. He would use quite a few before he was finished with Bill Thomas that night.

"Listen, Lou," said Bill, "I want you to know that I didn't mean to kill him or anything."

"Hey," said Lou, trying the best he knew how to console him, "these things happen."

"Yeah, I know, but I mean it wasn't a life and death type situation or anything. I mean all I really wanted to do was just glance him or something. He was a great guy."

"Sure, Bill, sure," said Lou as he signaled the doctor to give Bill something to calm him down. "Don't get too upset... it could've just as easily been you."

"Yeah, I know, but it wasn't. I feel really bad, that's all Lou. Really bad."

The doctor gave Bill an injection of morphine. He quieted down.

The main barroom of the Club was filled to capacity with the post-fight crowd. Drinks were being served and bets were being paid while the fight was being re-fought for the twentieth time. This ritual usually continued well past midnight, but on a night when one of the contestants had died the conversations could sometimes last well into the morning. Some of the members were watching a videotape replay. This had been a particularly unusual fight inasmuch as there were very few deaths in one on one knife combat. Mostly wounds. Also, as Jones had been a favorite at the Club, having been successfully fighting there for over four years, his loss was cause for considerable debate. Had it been luck? Had it been skill? Was it that Thomas was such a vastly superior fighter, or was it simply a case of Jones having had the misfortune of walking into an untimely placed knife? It would be hours before anyone would begin retiring to their rooms or leaving for home.

Bill Thomas would receive $250,000 for the fight he had just fought. It would be paid directly into a numbered account that was maintained in his name in Zurich. This had been Bill's eighth fight at the Club. It was the second time that one of his fights had resulted in the death of an opponent. He had won all eight fights and had inflicted as well as received numerous wounds.

The Club maintained a small house on an isolated island off of Connecticut. It was here that fighters who had been seriously wounded enough to require health care were sent. Bill was in a bed in this house within an hour and a half of the fight's conclusion. He would stay here for at least two weeks. He would also undergo cosmetic surgery here for his shattered nose and the slash that Jones had given his cheek. All in all it was a pleasant place to recuperate. A little boring and quiet perhaps, but inasmuch as it was only the second time that Bill had had to spend time there he wasn't very upset. Yes, he would have preferred that sunny Caribbean beach he had anticipated... but that could wait.

Bill was originally from the midwest. He had grown up in a large family that was very well grounded in the traditions of American life. He had had four brothers and three sisters and their family had always had to eat in shifts. His father was a clerk in a bank. Slightly less prestigious than if he had been an accountant, but basically the same work. His mother ran a small dancing school in the basement of their house. There weren't many children who had grown up in their town without having taken some kind of dancing lessons from "Miss Ritter". Bill's brothers and sisters had all grown up pretty much according to plan. His sisters were all married and raising families of their own and his brothers were all in business or adequately employed. Bill ran away from home when he was fifteen. He hadn't seen any of his family since that time twenty years ago. He never wondered how they were.

He joined the navy, lying about his age, and stayed there for five years. He liked it a lot. Much more so than his home life. When he finally quit it was only because he wanted to switch services. He thought it would be fun to spend a little time on land. He enlisted in the army under another name. He fought in Vietnam. He was never wounded and was never awarded any citations. He didn't kill anyone either. He did, however, find that he was very much at ease in a situation where the majority of those around him were scared to death. After he left the army he applied for jobs with a number of enforcement agencies. He was turned down by both the FBI and the CIA. His education was severely deficient and they did not consider him to be particularly qualified. The police was definitely out of the question. Not glamorous enough.

In 1974 he came into contact with a mercenary group through an ad in a magazine. He applied for work and was accepted. He fought in Africa for a year and a half. The pay was excellent. It was here that he first heard about the Club. Through connections that he had made while in Africa he wound up in New York where he was interviewed by the Selection Committee. He was given physical tests and subjected to an extensive background search. When he was finally approved as a potential combatant he was explained the financial arrangements and the contractual obligations to which he would be held. He agreed to them all and was given a new name and identity. He was also advanced $100,000 and given his first apartment. Bill really enjoyed his life. He had no complaints.

Ever since the night that Bill had thrown him out John had been going through a terrible depression. He had really been hooked on Bill and had thought that the feeling had been mutual. Obviously he had been mistaken. At first his resentment sent him cruising the West Village bars. After all, what the hell did he care about some jerk with a build? There were only twenty just like him in every joint in town. For three days he was with somebody new every night, but he never really stopped thinking about Bill. He remembered the tenderness and concern. He remembered the closeness that they had felt. How could that have not been real? How could Bill have faked something like that? Better yet, *why* would he have faked something like that? If he could just see him and talk things over, he decided, everything could probably be worked out. If he could only get Bill to explain to him exactly what it was that had put him off he would be willing to change it if he could. He tried to call Bill on the telephone but found that the number had been disconnected. He went over to his building and was told that Bill had given up his apartment and moved all of his things out. Did they know where he had gone? They did not. Had he left a forwarding address? He had not.

Once, when they were still together, Bill had walked John to work. He was on his way to the gym he had said and had left John at the corner of Sixth Avenue and 53rd Street. They had said goodbye and Bill had disappeared into the crowd. While he was waiting for the light to change John had looked over his shoulder and briefly seen Bill emerge from the crowd and enter the service portal of the Northrop Tower. He was surprised at the location but assumed that this must be the entrance to the gym where Bill spent most of his time. He decided to ask for him there. He didn't care if he was demeaning himself. He had a right.

Bill was lying on his back watching the television that was suspended from the ceiling in front of his bed. He had gotten into the soaps lately and was watching "The Edge of Night" when Lou Geller knocked briskly at the door.

"Hey, Bill, how are you?" he asked.

"Lou," said Bill sitting up, "you old rascal, how you doing? Boy, is it grcat to scc you."

"Yeah," said Lou facetiously, "you sure look great." Bill's face was covered with bandages. His arms and legs were wrapped.

"Oh yeah?" said Bill, raising his arm as if he were going to hit him. "I'll still take you two out of three falls."

"This is the only time I can think of where I might take you up on that." They both laughed.

"So, what's the story, Lou? What's happening?"

"Oh, you know, the regular." He looked around the room.

"Anything interesting up?"

"Nothing much. I think they might be setting something up with Alex and that new guy."

"Who? Fenn? Hey, Alex'll kill him!"

"Yeah," said Lou, "maybe, maybe not."

"C'mon, Lou, you're crazy... he'll kill that guy! I'd sure like to see that!"

"So get better and you will."

"Yeah," said Bill, "I guess so."

"Hey, Bill, you know they got you a new apartment," said Lou. He picked up a newspaper that was lying on the floor.

"Whattaya mean? What was wrong with the old one?"

"Nothing, I guess, but those are the rules." He flipped a couple of pages. "Hey, what kinda crap is this?"

"That's for intellectuals, not jerks like you. Shit, Lou, I happened to like that place."

"Well, anyway, I wouldn't worry too much about it, my intellectual friend," said Lou. "They found you another beauty. Yeah, and I hear this one's got a library with all the Hardy Boy books in it for when you finish this *Moneysworth* gizmo." He threw the paper on the floor.

"Yeah," said Bill, "well, we'll see about that."

"Yeah," said Lou, "I guess we will."

Bill pushed the button on the changer and started switching channels. He stopped at another soap.

"Hey, Lou, you ever watch this stuff?"

"Oh c'mon, willya!"

They both watched the screen for awhile. They

didn't speak. Finally Lou broke the silence.

"Say, Bill, do you know a guy named John Shasky?"

Bill continued to watch the screen. He didn't register a reaction. "I don't know. Why?"

"Well, only because he's been asking around after you."

"So what?" said Bill. "Let him ask all he wants."

"Yeah, but he keeps coming down by the Club asking all kindsa questions."

Bill started. "By the Club. Whattaya mean by the Club? How would he know where the Club is?"

"That's what I'm supposed to ask you."

"Supposed to ask me. Shit, Lou, what is this, the third degree," said Bill. He laughed. "I don't know how he found out where the Club is, but you can bet that's all he knows. I don't tell nobody nothing." He changed the channel again. "And, anyway, he's just some guy I know. What the hell does he care anyway?"

"Well, I don't know, Bill. But, he sure has been poking around. A couple of the guys told him to get lost and that nobody knew where you were. But, then he stops a couple of the members out on the street and starts bugging them."

"Oh shit, Lou." Bill turned on his side. His back was facing Lou. He looked out the window. He could see the water.

"Yeah, and then he tells one of these guys that if he doesn't find out what happened to you he's gonna go to the police. This guy's making a real problem here. You know how nervous the members get."

"So, what do you want me to do about it anyway?" Both men were silent again. In the background somebody on the television was talking about somebody's open heart surgery. Somebody was always having some kind of an operation, thought Bill.

"Hey, Bill."

"Yeah?"

"Don't get the wrong idea or anything, but what is this guy, some kinda faggot or what?"

"Whattaya mean?"

"Well, I mean this guy is some kinda queer or something. He's got an earring, y'know, and all that stuff."

"Hey, Lou, I don't know what the hell the guy is. Why don't you ask him yourself."

There was a long pause. "This guy isn't your lover or something, is he?"

"Oh shit, Lou, gimme a break, willya."

"Well, there was a time not so very long ago when my major beliefs hovered somewhere in the general vicinity of peace on Earth, good will towards men..." Henry Ostling leaned back broadly in his chair. He had long since, during the course of this interview, adopted a look of deep pensiveness. It was a luxury he could obviously well afford. It wasn't every man that was called upon to give a recounting of his life and views for a national publication.

"And now?" asked Mark Flynn.

"Well, now, and please don't misunderstand me, Mr. Flynn... I'm as much for peace as the next man... but, it seems to me that a certain amount of healthy conflict among men is just what the doctor ordered."

"Um-hmm."

"On the one hand, peace is the thing that we most desire. The aim that most men and governments aspire to, but on the other hand it almost seems contrary to God's law. It almost strikes me sometimes as being counter-productive to Man's goals. Counter-productive to his ambitions and interests."

"That's very interesting," said Flynn.

"But, I'm boring you," offered Ostling unctuously.

"No," said Flynn, picking up the cue, "not at all. On the contrary I find your theories fascinating. Please go on."

"Well, you see, Mark, I've read a great deal of history and have made a lifelong layman's study of Man and his civilization... let me ask *you* a question." Flynn nodded. "When is it that Man is the most productive? When is it that Man creates the most inspired of his works? From what one common denominator do some of the most important elements of Man's civilization and greatness arise? From conflict!" Ostling removed his glasses for effect. Flynn looked dutifully impressed.

"The truth is, you see, Mark, that Man is a combatant by nature. He is a competitor who functions the best under pressure. He's a fighter. It's that sense of danger and contest that keeps him on edge. That keeps him ready, thinking and working. I know. I'm that way myself. That's how I got to the top of the heap in this business. I fought tooth and nail to get where I am and I saw a lot of good men go down on the way. It made me fight harder. It made me want to get there that much more. If there is one word of advice that I would offer to any young man starting out in life, any young man, like yourself, that wants all that this life has to offer, it would be to fight. Fight! That would be what I'd tell him."

Flynn switched off his tape recorder and nodded. He nodded and smiled.

John Shasky finished the beer that he'd been sipping for almost an hour and looked at his watch for the fortieth time. He was upset, nervous and anxious. What the hell was going on up there? He was about to signal the waitress when he saw Mark Flynn come through the door. He waved to him.

"Hey, Mark, over here!"

Flynn, seeing him, dramatically wiped his hand across his brow. He worked his way through the after-office-hours crowd to John's table.

"Oh brother, John, you sure can pick 'em! This guy is a lulu!"

"Yeah?"

"Unbelievable when you think that he controls one of the richest companies in the country. Just goes to show you. I oughta ask for a refund on my Masters degree, because it obviously isn't going to do me any good."

"So what happened?" John was getting impatient.

"We had a lovely talk. We talked about flowers and movies and walks in the park and cutting the balls off any poor slob that might happen to get in your way. And, all in the name of humanity, if that don't beat all! This guy's got it all worked out. He's serving Mankind better than any of the rest of us and he's doing it by crushing people's lives and careers left and right as he goes along. It creates a healthier economy. The amazing thing, and it gets worse as we go along, is that he believes every word of it. You never saw a guy happier to finally have a chance to air his philosophical dirty laundry. As far as he's concerned he's a fucking saint! Here, listen to this later." He handed him the tape recorder. Then, taking the last sip of beer from the glass in front of him, he leaned a little closer to John. "You know something, bubula, your old Uncle Mark has a sixth sense for this kind of stuff, and you can take it from me... this one is hot."

The Club was on edge that evening. Alex Nogrady, a regular favorite for four years, was scheduled to fight Tom Fenn. Fenn was a new fighter that had only recently been recruited. This would be his first fight. He had shown exceptional promise in the three months he'd been training at the gym and the smart money was even all around. Fenn was flashy and strong, but Alex still had the experience. And in the long run it was very often the experience that determined the outcome. They would be fighting with nets and maces which was another unusual element in this bout. Generally they were not allowed in matches that were the first time out for either participant. Too much damage. But, in this case, there had been a certain degree of animosity that had developed between Alex and Fenn during training and sparring sessions. This was always frowned upon and discouraged as best as possible, but when it was unavoidable it was allowed to run its course. It made for a hell of a fight.

Bill Thomas walked through the door of the main auditorium escorted by Lou Geller. There were still bandages on his face and arm, and he was walking with a cane. A number of the members and some of the fighters, those that were in their street clothes and just there to watch the fight, met them at their seats.

"Hey, Bill, how are you?"

"You're looking great!"

"God, was that a fight! I'll remember that one as long as I live!"

Bill was beaming. It felt good to be back.

"Bill, my boy." Henry Ostling put his hand on Bill's shoulder. Bill turned in his seat to face him.

"Hello, sir, how are you?"

"Me?" Henry laughed. "I'm fine! Much more to the point, how are you?"

"Oh, I'm fine, Mr. Ostling. Everything's healing

real well."

"That's great... that's really great." He patted Bill's shoulder. Bill smiled.

"Listen, Bill... a couple of the boys and I were wondering if you wouldn't mind having a drink with us after the fight."

"Well sure, Mr. Ostling... it'd be my pleasure."

"Oh, that's great... that's wonderful. Why don't you just meet us up in the Board Room then, alright."

"Yes, sir."

"Can you make it up there by yourself?" he asked, glancing sidelong at Lou.

"Yes, sir, I'm sure I can."

Ostling smiled and patted Bill on the shoulder again. "That's the boy... we'll see you later, then."

He winked at Bill as he left.

"I guess this is where the shit hits the fan, huh, Lou."

"Naw, I think he just wants to give you a medal or something."

"Yeah."

There was a preliminary fight before Nogrady and Fenn would come on. It was to be fought freestyle without weapons. These fights were never fatal, usually amounting to nothing more than a broken arm or nose. But, they were considered a tremendous amount of fun and always worked the crowd up to a wonderful pitch before the main event.

Tonight this preliminary was being fought by two of the younger fighters. They were both about eighteen and were not yet allowed to fight with weapons. By the time they were, however, they would both be two year veterans of the Club and should have become very formidable opponents.

The fight was not a long one and betting on it was not very heavy. The majority of the spectators were still milling around talking with each other while many were still in the bar having a last minute smoke and a drink. The fighters' attention was much more concentrated than their audience's. They had been well trained since coming to the Club. Both had been street fighters in their early teens. Allen Druss was from the Bronx and Cornelius Francis was from Jamaica in the West Indies. The combination of the different street fighting techniques that they both knew from home and the more classical training that they had received since joining the Club made for a very satisfactory clash. There was a little bit of everything thrown in. Some boxing, some karate, some judo, some aikido and some just plain old dirty fighting. For every hold that one of them would get on the other there was a bite, kick or a gouge that would get him out. After about five minutes of generally throwing each other around Druss got Cornelius in a bar hammerlock and was trying to take him down to the ground with it. For his efforts he received a lovely smash on the instep of his foot and a fist in the groin. When he doubled over Cornelius grabbed him by the back of the neck and smashed Allen's head down into his upraised knee. It was a pretty short fight.

"C'mon," said Lou, "whattaya say we get a drink."

Bill picked up his cane and, with a little help from Lou, they walked over to the barroom. Three of the fighters were sitting at a table near the entrance to the room and as Lou and Bill passed by one of them let out a distinct kissing sound. They kept walking.

"Hey, Lover Boy!" The three men laughed.

"Eat shit, Simpson."

"Wow," said Simpson, "I heard you guys do some weird things, but not that!" The three men laughed again. Lou tightened his grip on Bill's arm and continued to lead him towards a table in the rear. "Let it slide, Bill. He's just an asshole anyway."

"Hey, Thomas!" Simpson was getting loud. "I can't wait till you're back in action... I got some things I want to talk over with you in the shower!" He squeezed his groin suggestively. His buddies loved it.

"Yeah, why don't we talk it over on the mats instead!" Bill raised his cane as if to hit him. Simpson jumped to his feet.

"Anytime, you stupid faggot!"

"Hey, guys," said Lou insinuating himself between them. "Whattaya say we calm down here, huh. The fight's in the other room."

"Ahh, stupid faggot..."

"Hey, Simpson," said Lou, "why don't you just sit back down before I have to fine you or something."

"Je-sus!" said Simpson.

"Stupid shit," said Bill.

"C'mon, Bill." Lou led him to the free table in the

27

rear. They ordered a couple of beers.

"Hey, Bill, so whadya think of that colored guy?"

"Shit! That fuckin' Simpson..." Bill was still looking at the table of fighters. They laughed in his direction.

"C'mon, forget it. What the hell do you care what an asshole like that thinks? So whadya think of that Cornelius Francis guy?"

"Huh?"

"That colored guy in the other fight. Whadya think of him?"

"Oh say, Lou, he was great... no kidding. Lotsa promise!"

"Yeah," said Lou smiling, "that's what I think, too."

"Yeah," said Bill, "lotsa promise."

"Yeah, I was hoping to get you two together for a little training when you're back in commission."

"Sure thing, Lou... that'd be great."

"Yeah, you could really show him a few things."

"Yeah," said Bill. He was still watching the other table. A buzzer sounded indicating the start of the main event. The bar emptied as people scattered to find seats.

Nets and maces carried with them a special show as the combatants always wore, by choice, gladiatorial costumes. Some of the members thought it was a little hokey, but the majority loved it.

Alex was the first to come through the swinging doors off the auditorium. He was carrying a net and mace and was wearing knee high sandals, a leather breastplate and a steel helmet. Tom Fenn followed behind shortly. He, too, carried his mace and net and was also wearing sandals, breastplate and helmet. They were both attended by seconds.

Tony Campisi, a short, round man in a tuxedo, walked to the center of the mat. He had been refereeing the fights at the Club for over fifteen years. He took a piece of paper from his pocket, unfolded it carefully and began to read.

"Gentlemen," he called in a high voice, "tonight we are going to witness a match with nets and maces. The contestants in this match are, on my left, Alex Nogrady... he is six feet two inches tall and weighs 225 pounds. He has fought eighteen fights at the Club, and has won 12, drawn 3 and lost 3." There was a long burst of applause from the audience. It continued until Tony raised his paper in the air for quiet. He continued. "And, on my right, Mr. Tom Fenn. He is six feet tall and weighs 195 pounds. Tonight will be his first fight at the Club. We wish him excellent luck." There was another burst of applause. All around the room bets were being placed as the crowd sized up the two men. Tony again raised his paper. "Gentlemen..." he looked first at Nogrady and then at Fenn. They joined him in the center of the mat. "Gentlemen, there are no rules or regulations in this competition, save that we insist you confine your activities to the matted areas." There was a laugh in the audience. Tony continued. "There will be two periods of ten minutes each.

In between there will be a rest period of five minutes. Do you understand?" They bòth nodded. "Please shake hands, then, and prepare yourselves." The men shook hands and returned to their respective corners. The room was quiet as they awaited the bell. Both contestants discussed last minute strategies with their seconds. The bell rang.

Nogrady advances quickly to the center of the mats. Fenn approaches him slowly. They circle each other cautiously as each man watches for the correct moment to make his move. Fenn makes a half-hearted pass at Alex with his net. Nogrady catches it on his own. They disentangle and step away from each other. Nogrady is left handed and both men are carrying their nets on the same side. Fenn is aware of the disadvantage that this creates for him. Nogrady is more used to fighting right handed opponents than Fenn is to fighting left handed ones. They continue to circle. A man in the audience breaks the silence.

"C'mon, Fenn, get in there!" Alex, completely without warning, sweeps his net across the mat at Fenn's ankles. He momentarily knocks him off balance. He swings at him with his mace. Fenn catches the blow half on the shaft of his own mace and half on the metal wrist and hand guards that he is wearing. He is visibly shaken by how soon he has found himself at a disadvantage, but still manages to roll over his own shoulder in a somersault that takes him far enough away from Nogrady to regain his feet. He shakes his net out and they again begin to circle each other. Lou poked Bill in the ribs. "That Fenn's fast, huh. Another guy wouldn'ta got away so easy."

"Yeah," said Bill, "he's fast."

Alex presses his advantage and moves in on Fenn again. He swings his net and Fenn retreats. He swings again and Fenn retreats. The third time he swings Fenn drops his own net and grabs Nogrady's. He pulls him hard and swings with his mace. It connects with Alex's helmet which absorbs most of the impact. Alex still looks stunned. Fenn kicks him in the stomach as he passes. The audience likes this play. They never hesitate to voice their approval. The two men begin to circle each other again. Fenn is trying to work his way back to the area where he dropped his net. Nogrady is trying his best to keep him away from it. At what seems like a fairly safe moment, Fenn dives for the net, scoops it up and is long out of the way before Nogrady's mace passes him and hits the mat. It rips a large hole where it strikes. As they start to circle again the bell rings. They retreat to their corners. Despite the two or three minutes of action it had been a pretty dull first period. There were some decidedly rude catcalls from the crowd.

During the five minute break which followed, the bar again filled up rapidly. A number of new bets were made and even some outside business was discussed. Not surprisingly, there was a tremendous number of business deals that took place between members of the Club. They were very loyal to each other. When the buzzer indicating thirty seconds to the bell sounded the bar emptied.

As the bell rang the two men moved swiftly to the center of the matted area. They were understandably cautious as they both knew quite well the damage that could be inflicted by the weapons they were using. Fenn swung his mace and Nogrady parried it. He swung it again and it was again parried. They almost seemed to be dueling. As his third blow was parried Fenn swung his net from the side and succeeded in tangling Nogrady's net arm. Nogrady turns towards his tangled side and Fenn swings hard and fast and hits him full in the side and back. The spikes of his mace pierce Nogrady's breastplate and blood can be seen. It is only a superficial blow, but psychologically it has a lot of power for Fenn. He throws the end of his net that is still in his hand over Nogrady's opposite shoulder and manages to hit him with a glancing blow that rips some of the skin off his arm. Nogrady retreats to the other side of the mat. He removes both nets from his arm and drops them on the ground. Grabbing his mace in both hands and screaming at the top of his lungs, he attacks full force. Fenn blocks each swing as best he can, but Nogrady obviously has no intention of letting up. He just keeps swinging. The crowd picks up his energy and rises, yelling, to its feet. Nogrady keeps swinging. The shaft of Fenn's mace breaks as he takes what must be the tenth overhead blow on it. Nogrady draws back and hits him in the side with a shot that sends him reeling across the room. He lies still and bleeding as Nogrady races towards him. As he nears the prostrate figure voices in the audience begin calling for him to let the fallen man alone. The general consensus seems to be that he has had enough and it is with no small effort that Nogrady is able to quiet himself. Fenn is clearly not going to continue. He seems to be unconscious. He could be thankful that the worst he had probably suffered was a few broken ribs and some lacerations. It could have been much worse. Bill knew where Fenn would be spending the next couple of weeks. He hoped he liked the soaps. Nogrady paraded around the auditorium to thunderous applause. He held his mace high over his head.

"Come in," came a voice from inside. Bill opened the door to the Board Room. Henry Ostling stood up from the seat that he held at the head of the table.

"Ah, Bill, my boy... there you are. Come in, come in. I believe you know everyone." Bill nodded to the three other men in the room. "Here you go, Bill, have a seat." Ostling pulled the seat which was at the foot of the table out for him and gestured for him to sit. He returned to his own.

"Well," began Ostling, "first let me say what a tremendous job we all feel you did out there, Bill. I know I speak for the others when I say that we consider you to be our number one team member around here." The other men all nodded their agreement.

"And, I don't mind telling you," said Dick Alston, "I was able to put away a tidy little sum as a result of that fight."

"Oh, is that right, Mr. Alston?" asked Bill, politely raising his eyebrows.

"Unfortunately you haven't been around to see it," said Malcolm Anderson, "but he's been springing for drinks left and right off of your efforts."

Bill laughed.

"Yes, but I doubt if Murray is feeling quite so warmly towards you, Bill, since he lost most of the money I picked up."

"Is that right?" Bill laughed again. Murray Weissman smiled.

"Hey, Bill," said Ostling, "where are our manners? What'll you have?"

"Oh, a gin and tonic'd be fine, thanks."

Ostling pushed a button under the table and ordered the drink from a waiter who immediately came through a swinging door behind him. The five men remained silent as he mixed the drink at a small bar in the room, gave it to Bill and then left. Bill took a sip and tried, as best he could, to sneak a quick look at the faces of the Board Members as he tipped his head back.

"Well, Bill, let's not beat around the bush," said Ostling. Bill put his drink down on the table. "I guess you've figured out by now that we want to talk over this John Shasky business."

Bill didn't respond.

"It seems that this *friend* (Bill couldn't help noticing

34

the emphasis he placed on that word) of yours has, for some reason or another, taken a great deal of interest in our operation here."

"So Lou was telling me."

"He's been nosing around asking all kinds of questions, stopping members on the street, myself included I might add, and in general making an all around pest of himself."

"Um-hmm." Bill shifted in his seat. He took another sip of his drink.

"Bill, why don't you tell us exactly what you think is going on here."

"Well, sir, this Shasky is just some guy I was friendly with for awhile. I mean it's not like he's my best friend or anything, y'know." The men nodded. "Well, I guess he kinda formed some kind of an attachment or something, and when he hasn't heard from me he starts looking around. I don't know... maybe he even followed me down here one day or something."

"That certainly wasn't very prudent on your part, Bill," said Dick.

"I know, Mr. Alston, but I gotta tell you who ever woulda thought that the guy would be following me or anything, y'know?"

"Bill," began Malcolm, "I don't know... perhaps we've been terribly lucky in the past, but in the twenty-five years since this club was founded this is the first time that anything of this nature has happened."

"I'm really sorry," said Bill.

"Bill..."

"Yes, Mr. Ostling."

"I would think by this time that we've made you a very wealthy man."

"I can't complain..." They all laughed.

"In fact, by now I would think that you should probably be a millionaire."

Bill nodded.

"Well, even though we've all arrived at our material position in different ways it still makes us bunk mates of a sort. We should be beginning to understand each other much better by now. We start to share the same problems if you know what I mean."

"Yes, sir."

"Well then, Bill... what do we do about this little 'situation'?"

Bill picked up his drink again. He waited a few seconds before proceeding. He had already given the matter a great deal of thought and had pretty much decided what the best and simplest course of action would be. It couldn't hurt, though, to let these men think that it had just come off the top of his head.

"Well," he said, "how about if I get in touch with this Shasky like I just heard he was looking for me."

"Um-hmm." Ostling looked at him to continue.

"Well, here I am all bandaged up and everything. How about if I tell him I was in a car accident and I was in the hospital for the last couple of weeks."

"And your apartment?" asked Malcolm.

"Well, I could tell him that I took a job offer with a company in, say, Chicago, and I had to pack up everything and leave on a moment's notice. I'll tell him that I'd planned to write him after everything had gotten settled, but the next thing you know I haven't been in Chicago two days when I have this accident."

"Go on."

"Well, so after I get out of the hospital I'm feeling a lot better and I decide to head back to New York to pick up some of my stuff and finish straightening things out. In fact... I won't even tell him that I heard he was looking for me. Yeah, that's it. I'll just call him up like I just wanted to say hi and then tell him the whole story. If he says he's been looking for me I'll just act surprised. Hey, those guys over there wouldn't know where I went. It's just a gym where I work out. I hardly ever even spoke to anyone over there anyway." He leaned back in his chair. He was resting his case and figured it was a pretty good one.

Ostling took a deep breath and leaned back in his chair, too. He reached in his pocket for a pack of cigarettes. He was about to take one out, but threw the pack on the table in front of him instead. "Bill," he said, "would you excuse us for a few minutes?"

"Oh, sure," said Bill. "No problem." He got up slowly, intentionally emphasizing his dependency on the cane he was carrying, and went out into the hall. After only half a minute or so the door opened and Malcolm asked him back in.

"Okay, Bill," said Ostling, "we'll buy it... you go speak to this *friend* of yours." There was that word again. Bill said thanks and left.

II

Mark Flynn lived in a beautiful loft in SoHo. At least *he* thought it was beautiful. It satisfied all of his needs, had tons of space, was private, convenient, cheap and, anyway, who cared about a little dirt. The trucks and warehouses that lined the streets during the daytime didn't bother him either. Flynn considered trucks to be an American art form. He loved being surrounded by art. Girls always liked his apartment at first—it was earthy—and learned to hate it later. So it goes.

Flynn was at the moment, as was too often the case, thoroughly immersed in the tangles of a triangular love affair. He had a girl that he had been seeing for quite some time who was not aware of the fact that he was seeing another woman who, coincidentally, had a boyfriend who was not aware that she was seeing another man. The intrigue was thrilling, the hassle phenomonal and he was expecting that any day now his new friend would start to get sick of his filthy apartment anyway. Gee, but life was swell.

Nina Fischer, the girlfriend of the other boyfriend, was over for dinner. Mark had been telling her about his friend John Shasky and what had been going on since John had first told him about his missing lover.

"See, John and I grew up together in Washington. We've known each other since we were kids. We did everything together. Then, after we got out of college,

John moved out to San Francisco for two years and the next thing you know he's back and announcing to the world that he's become bisexual. He takes the rather inauspicious occasion of an intimate reunion dinner to tell me. I thought he was putting the make on me. I nearly shat in my pants! I mean, this guy was the biggest womanizer I ever knew! Two years later he's given up women for good and now he's exclusively gay! And we went to grade school together, too... how can that be!?"

Nina, who was standing by the oven trying to make some kind of sense out of Mark's disarrayed kitchen, laughed. Mark started jumping all over the place in his excitement.

"Hey, no, really... don't laugh." She cracked up. "This is serious! This guy is living in the West Village running all over the streets like some bitch in heat, cruising bath houses like some kind of refugee from Sodom and Gomorrah. I had lunch with him the other day and almost turned into a pillar of salt just looking at him!" Nina was dying. Mark grabbed her around the waist and started to tickle her.

"Cut it out, you asshole!" she screamed.

"Me? Me cut it out! My oldest friend is sinking into the depths of depravity, you're laughing your Goddamn balls off, and *I* should cut it out! Ladies and Gentlemen, I ask you... is this fair? Is this just? Oh... what a cruel world we live in!" He threw himself onto the couch in mock exasperation. The truth was he had just worn himself out. The phone rang and Mark reached for it. He knocked it on the floor.

"Hey! Hello, don't go away," he yelled at the receiver as he scrambled after it. "Hold on... I'm coming!" He grabbed it. "Hello?"

"Hey, Mark, how you doing?"

"Ho ho, John, what's happening? We were just laughing... I mean talking about you and your sexual proclivities."

"My ears were burning."

"Yeah, I'll bet." They both laughed. "So what's happening, you old rapscallion, you? Boy, have I got some stuff to tell you."

"Yeah, well wait till you hear what I have to tell you first."

"Yeah?"

"You'll never believe who just called me up."

"Yeah, who?" Flynn grabbed for Nina's ass as she walked by the couch.

"My missing friend in the flesh... Bill Thomas. I was on the phone with him for over an hour."

Flynn sat up slowly. "You're kidding?"

"No, I'm serious. He called and he's fine."

"So, where's he been all this time?"

"Oh shit, it turns out I was making such a mountain out of a molehill."

"Yeah?"

"He had to move to Chicago to take a job he'd been waiting to hear about for over a month. When they finally accepted him he had to leave on a day's notice."

"Yeah, so how come no word?"

41

"Well, one thing and another mounted up and the next thing you know he's in Chicago and hasn't even had a chance to let anyone know. He was planning to call me, but before he even has a chance to he smashes up this car he rented out there and boom he's off to the hospital."

"No kidding. Is he okay?"

"Oh yeah, he's fine. He busted his nose though, and he cracked a couple of ribs, but he'll be okay."

"Well, that's good."

"Yeah, he's in town, too, tying up some loose ends, so we're going to have dinner together tomorrow night."

"Well, just be careful you don't re-break any of those ribs, hee hee."

"Yeah, I'll be real gentle," said John. They both laughed.

"Well," said Mark, "so, that's really great."

"Yeah, it is," said John. "I guess I'll let you get back to whoever... I mean, whatever you were doing. I just wanted to let you know that everything was okay and that we could call the whole thing off now."

"What do you mean, call it off?" asked Flynn.

"I mean call it off. The guy's okay. There's nothing going on."

"Nothing going on!? What're you crazy or what?" Flynn loved to get excited. "That whole thing down there has got to be the fishiest set-up I've ever seen! I've got photographs of some of the heaviest hitters in New York coming out of that back door!"

"Well, Bill told me it's just a gymnasium. Those guys just work out there."

"Hey, let me tell you something, you're crazy! The only time any of those guys work out anything is from behind a desk! Listen, I've got an 8 x 10 glossy of a guy on a stretcher coming out of that place at four in the morning, so I don't know what the hell you're talking about!"

"So a guy has a stroke. Big deal! You know something, man, you're just getting all worked up about nothing. Really. There isn't anything going on over there except our imaginations."

"Listen, mi amigo, it just so happens that I'm looking to win some kind of a Pulitzer Prize with this baby. I'm telling you, this one is hot!"

"Give me a break, will you, Flynn. Some guy lets you into his drop dead gorgeous office, talks a lot of right wing crap and you're ready to march out the troops. Do me a favor, will you... just call the whole thing off."

"No way, José. I already did you a favor when I started looking into this whole thing. I'm not calling anything off. Too late!" He slammed the phone down, then reached for it again. Nina put her hand over his.

"Mark, you haven't got anything in the kitchen. Let's go out and get something to eat."

"C'mon in the bedroom... I got something we can eat in there!" He attacked.

John Shasky was sitting at the bar of Leo's, a small restaurant in the Village that had been a favorite of Bill's when they had been together. It was John who had suggested that they dine there. He wanted everything to be just right. He perked up as Bill Thomas walked through the door.

"Hey, John, how are you?" He held out his hand. John stood and threw his arms around Bill. He was feeling wonderfully emotional.

"Oh, Bill, you're a mess!" Bill pulled back from him. He didn't really want John hugging him. Especially not in public. He tried to make it look like he was just stepping back to give him room to survey the damage. God, this was all very embarrassing.

"Oh, it's not as bad as all that. I'm healing real well and I should be out of all this junk in no time. Hey, but you look great."

"Who me?" said John. He smiled and shrugged. "I never change."

"Yeah. Well, let's get something to eat around here. I'm starving."

They took a small table in the corner. John made sure Bill got the seat facing into the room. He knew Bill loved to watch the other people in a restaurant.

"So tell me about the accident," he said. "Exactly what happened?"

"Well, there isn't much to tell. Some jerk in a Mercedes decides to go through a red light at thirty-five miles per hour and I happened to be the poor shnook that got caught in the middle."

"Ow!"

"Yeah. So, they took me to the hospital, patched me up, put me to bed for a couple of weeks, and the rest is all history." Bill shrugged. John's face was resting in his hands, his elbows leaning on the table. He was staring into Bill's eyes. He just couldn't seem to get enough of that face.

"So what happened to the guy in the other car?" he asked.

Bill looked a little surprised. He'd never thought about that. "Huh? Oh yeah, well to tell you the truth I don't even know!" He half laughed. "Can you believe it, I never even asked how the other guy was! He coulda killed himself for all I know!"

"Your concern is touching."

"Yeah."

They both picked up their menus and started reading.

"So what do you think looks good?" asked Bill.

"You," said John. Bill looked sick.

"I think I'm gonna get a cheeseburger or something."

"Yeah, me too," said John. Bill was starting to look nervous. He was having trouble looking John in the eyes. A waiter came over and took their order.

"You know, Bill, you can't imagine how worried I was."

"Oh yeah?"

"I looked everywhere for you. It was like you had just disappeared off the face of the earth."

"Hmmph." That was just proof, thought Bill, of how efficient the organization was.

"You can't imagine the kinds of things that were going through my mind. First the apartment and then everybody down at your gym saying they had never even heard of you."

"Yeah, how'd you ever happen to go down there anyway?" asked Bill. This, at least, he was interested in.

"I figured somebody down there would know where you were. I mean after all, you only spent half your waking hours over there!"

"No, but I mean, how'd you even know where the place was? I never took you down there or anything, did I?"

"Oh, one day when you walked me down to work I saw you go into the entrance on the side of that building. I wasn't spying on you or anything. I got caught at the light longer than I should have and happened to look over my shoulder. I wanted to catch a last look at that cute ass of yours."

Shit, thought Bill, I wish he'd cut that crap out. "So, it turned out you had nothing to worry about after all, huh," he laughed.

"Yeah, I guess so."

The waiter brought their food and they both stopped talking until he had gone. Bill took a bite of his cheeseburger. John didn't touch his.

"Do you remember my talking about my friend Mark Flynn?"

"Yeah," said Bill, "I guess so."

"He's the guy I grew up with who writes freelance for magazines."

"Oh yeah, I remember."

"Well, it got so bad at one point that my suspicions just started running away with me. So I got Mark to help me and we actually started 'staking out' your gym." He laughed loudly. He was sure Bill would get a kick out of that. Bill looked anything but amused.

"Is that right?"

"Yeah, and believe it or not, he got into it even more than I did! Well, he's crazy anyway."

"Oh yeah?"

"You wouldn't have believed him down there with two different kinds of cameras taking pictures of all these guys coming out."

"He took pictures?"

"Yeah," said John. "There was even this one guy that's the president of this huge company that Mark recognized and you know what he does?"

"No, what?"

John laughed. "This madman friend of mine actually calls up the guy's office, sets up an appointment and goes up there and interviews him!"

"C'mon, you're kidding!" Bill forced himself to chuckle.

"No, I'm serious. Hey, you've got to understand, Flynn sees conspiracies coming out of the walls. He was in the SDS when we were in college and all that crap."

"Sounds like a real character."

"That he is alright!"

Bill took another bite out of his burger and tried

to affect an air of genuine indifference.

"So I guess this crazy friend of yours was pretty disappointed when you told him what had really happened. Kinda shot all his investigating to hell, huh."

"Not Flynn! Uh-uhh! All you have to do is show him a dead horse and he'll beat it with a stick."

"Whattaya mean?"

"Oh, Flynn's a jerk... that's all. He never knows when to let well enough alone. I told him that everything was okay and all about what had happened to you, but he couldn't care less. He said he was going to keep on investigating the place anyway."

"What the hell for?" Bill seemed disturbed. John let it pass.

"Like I said, he's crazy. He swears there's something weird going on over there and he thinks he's going to win a Pulitzer Prize finding out what it is."

"Well, he oughta mind his own fucking business."

"Hey, Bill, what's the problem? If he wants to waste his time putzing around with stories that don't go anywhere, what the hell do we care?" He reached across the table and put his hand on Bill's. Bill pulled it away.

"I care... that's all."

Flynn was amazed. He had been a trashy movie buff all his life. He was perhaps the most dedicated and avid fan of pulp literature that had ever turned a page. Yet, somewhere in the back of his mind doubt as to

THE KING OF CLUBS

the veracity of his beloved tomes always seemed to
linger. How could such dialogue be true? How could
such situations really exist? Yet, here he was, flat on
his back, a living testimonial to the mystical link that
has always and would always exist between fact and
fiction. He felt like a real fool as Linda Hoskins,
his number one girlfriend who would not be quite so
generous with him if she knew he was seeing another
woman, applied an icepack to some of the more obvious
contusions on his face. She would have to get to the
more subtle ones later.

At 9 o'clock that evening Flynn had been coming
home from the grocery store. He had been just about
to open the front door of his building when a rather
large man approached him from his right side. He
asked Flynn if he had a match (Flynn winced as he
remembered that. What a tip-off! A match... oh
brother!). While Mark was fumbling with his packages
and trying to get a lighter from his pocket the man hit
him in the face with his fist. Mark dropped his packages and stumbled back against the building. Out of
nowhere three more men appeared and started to work
him over. Real 1940's grade-B type stuff. What would
Dick Powell have done at a time like this? He hoped
to God they wouldn't knock any of his teeth out. It
all happened so fast he hadn't even had time to collect
his thoughts. He couldn't move... he couldn't speak.
In what must have been thirty seconds but seemed
like a year, he was on the ground and receiving a last
affectionate kick in the ribs. The first man, the one

who had asked him for the light, reached down and grabbed him by the shirt. He lifted his chest up off the ground. "Maybe this'll teach you to keep your nose out of other people's business," he said, and let Flynn drop. Jesus, thought Mark, this can't be for real. If it hadn't been for the undeniable fact that he was lying in the street with the shit beaten out of him, he would have been sure that it was all just a practical joke. Probably broke his eggs, too.

Linda sat down next to Flynn and started to massage his shoulders. He groaned his appreciation.

"Boy," she said, "they really gave it to you, huh?"

"Yeah. You know, the funny thing is that it really is just like in the movies. If this hadn't happened I probably would have let the whole thing drop. I was only just killing time, anyway."

"Well, how do you know they were even talking about that gym story?" asked Linda. She was trying to steer him off the whole thing. She didn't like the story and she wasn't all that crazy about Mark's friend John.

"Because, the guy said that this would teach me to stop sticking my nose into other people's business."

"So?"

"So the truth is that that's the only other person's business that I've been sticking my nose into! It couldn't be anything else, because there isn't anything else! I'm not working on another Goddamn thing in the world!" He moaned as she hit a tender spot.

"Well, maybe it has to do with some other story you

already wrote," Linda offered. She could see where all of this was going to lead.

"Not a chance," said Flynn in as loud a voice as he could muster. He really wasn't feeling up to his usual bursts of temper. "The most controversial thing I've written in the last two years was about a garden some jerks in the East Village wanted to put into a vacant lot and how some of the other people in the neighborhood didn't want them to do it. I can't see anybody beating me up over that! At least not a year later. Maybe at the time... ahh, I don't know..."

"Why don't you take a nap and I'll start to make some dinner for us. You'll feel a lot better when you wake up."

"Yeah, why don't you make us a nice omelette? You can't, that's why! Because those fucking assholes broke all my fucking eggs!" The ice bag fell off his cheek and onto the floor as he started to fall asleep. Linda picked it up and put it back on his face.

"Why do men fight? Hey, who the hell knows? Everybody fights for different reasons. You got some guys that fight for food and shelter, and you got other guys that fight for their families. When you haven't got any of those things to fight for then you do it for relaxation. I mean, what's more fun than popping some guy in the nose whether he's got it coming to him or not? To me there's nothing more fun than a good barroom brawl. I won't know a soul in the place and I'll just walk right in and sock some guy in the puss and start a free-for-all. I've had times when I busted my best friend in the nose and he didn't even care. I mean we were still friends and all. You know, fighting's one thing and friendship's another."

Murray Weissman was in the bar talking with Jeff Simpson. He had cornered him that afternoon and invited him for a drink. He wanted to try and find out what made him tick. The last time he had seen Simpson was the night the Board had been telling him what to do about Mark Flynn. Both he and Anderson had been a little concerned that Simpson might get too tough with Flynn, but Ostling was quite sure that this wouldn't be the case. "The man," he had said, "is a professional. If he can't control himself in a situation like this, who can?"

"What about with that Flynn guy?" asked Murray. "What did you feel when you were doing that?"

"Oh, that... that was just a piece of cake. I mean he was just this little guy, y'know. I almost felt sorry for him."

"But you did it anyway."

"Yeah, sure."

Murray waved for the waiter. "You want another drink, Jeff?"

"Sure thing."

Murray raised his hand as the waiter approached and signaled that they wanted two more of the same. He turned back to Simpson.

"What really interests me, though, is what you're thinking about when you're on the mats."

"Oh, man, that's the best!"

"How do you mean?"

"Well, it just is. You're completely free, y'know? Half the time you might get killed... the other half you might kill somebody else. Everything's pumping. You're high as a kite. Hey, what can I say? It's real... living and dying is the real thing."

"But what about when you actually kill somebody? Doesn't that bother you?"

"Hell no," said Jeff. "Any guy on that mat knows what's happening. That's part of what it's all about. It might just as easily be me as him. Doesn't bother me at all. Hey, I've been ripped to shreds out there. Did you ever see some of the scars I've got here? Murray shook his head no. "Well, I don't want to be indecent, but just look at this one." He reached down and pulled up his shirt. There was a thick scar that ran diagonally across the entire surface of his stomach. "This guy ripped me open like a pig. I almost died from this one!"

"Yes, I know," said Murray, "I saw that fight."

"Well, then you know what I'm talking about," said Jeff triumphantly. "Look, I don't have to tell you about all of this stuff. You know exactly what I'm talking about. Or else, what are you doing here?" Murray shrugged his shoulders. "No kidding, Mr. Weissman, how about you? What do you get out of it?"

Murray thought about it. He always thought about

it. On the one hand he couldn't be more intellectually opposed to everything the Club stood for. The entire concept was abhorrent to him. It was like denying everything that was supposed to be civilized about Man. On the other hand it was one of the major elements in his life. When he sat back and calculated the amount of time and money he spent in an average year at the Club, he realized that it was, at this point, almost his sole reason for living. "I don't know exactly. I just love it. When I watch a match I'm alive. Everything inside of me seems to stand up and shout. There's nothing like it."

"So if it's just a good fight you like, why don't you go down to the Garden and watch some of them boxers? Those guys are great," chided Simpson.

"It's just not the same," said Murray. "You know that."

Jeff Simpson smiled. Of course he knew it. He always had known it and always would. He just loved to make these guys squirm.

"Hey, by the way, Mr Weissman. You're on the Board, right?"

"Yes."

"So why don't you guys set up a match between Bill Thomas and me?"

Murray's mind snapped back sharply to the Club. He didn't really wander all that often, but it made him feel better, more complex, to question himself like this periodically. "What are you talking about, Simpson?" he asked. "Thomas has got at least another month of recuping before he even starts training."

"I can wait."

"What do you want to fight Thomas for?" Murray asked. His interest was piqued.

"I hate faggots. I want to cut his faggot balls off."

"Oh hey, that's great, Simpson. You know we don't condone grudge matches."

"Hey, you got me all wrong, Mr. Weissman... I haven't got any kind of grudge... I just hate his fuckin' guts, that's all!" Jeff threw his head back and laughed loudly. Everybody in the bar turned to see what was so funny. Murray laughed, too.

Bill had had to call information in Glen Cove, Kansas for the telephone number. He certainly didn't have it anymore, and besides, he didn't even know if any of them still lived there. The listing was there. Same address. He didn't know if he should call the number or not. Maybe he should just let it lie. He didn't even have the slightest idea what had made him look it up. In twenty years he'd hardly ever thought of them once and now here he was on the verge of calling. Ah, what the hell, he'd dial the number. He could always hang up anyway.

The phone rang once, then twice. It had that scratchy, detached sound that long distance calls always have. Somebody answered the phone and said hello. Shit, he wasn't sure, but it sounded like his mother.

"Hello?" the voice repeated.

"Hello," said Bill quietly.

"Can 1 help you?"

"Uh, yeah, is this Mildred Wojcik?" he asked.

"Yes, it is..."

"Uh, Mom, this is Billy."

There was a long pause. Bill couldn't hear anything but that crackling static. He thought maybe he'd been cut off.

"Hello..." he said.

"Billy?" The voice was hushed, almost reverent.

"Yeah, Ma, it's me... how are you?"

"Oh my God! Billy! It can't be. Billy, we didn't even know if you were still alive!"

"Yeah," he laughed, "I'm alive alright. At least it looks that way!"

"Oh my God, Billy... where are you? Where have you been, what have you been doing?" Bill couldn't tell if she was laughing or crying.

"I'm in New York. That's where I live." Oh shit, he thought, I've gotta be more careful. "So, how's Pa? Is he okay?"

"Of course his is! He's just upstairs taking a nap. Wait a second, I'll call him..."

"No, Ma, that's okay. Listen, what I'd like to do is come out there and see you folks. Would that be okay?"

"Okay? My God, of course it would be okay! When can you come? How long can you stay?" She sounded very excited. It made him feel good.

"Well, I thought I'd catch a plane out and be there

for the weekend."

"This weekend! I'll have to start getting ready now!" She sounded so flustered.

"Well, if it's any trouble I could come another time." He was starting to feel a little weak in his resolve.

"Oh no, please, Billy, come this weekend! Please come this weekend!"

"Okay, Mom, I will... I'll call up and make a reservation right after I get off. Hey listen, how's everybody else? Is everybody alright?"

"Oh, Billy, everybody's fine... you're an uncle nine times over!"

"Nine times!" he laughed. "Is that right? Well hell then, Ma, I'll see you this weekend."

"Oh, Billy, I can't wait! This is the happiest day of my life." Bill could hear her starting to cry. He wanted to cut it short.

"Okay, Ma, look, don't cry. I have to go now, so I'll see you this weekend. You take care, now. Bye." He only barely heard her say goodbye as he hung up. He didn't know if he was really going to go. He'd see. He had until the weekend to decide anyway.

Flynn wasn't feeling particularly comfortable. Not comfortable enough at least to be going out. He had been locked up in his apartment for the past two days sending out to the deli for a steady stream of sandwiches and Coke. He had spent most of the time curled up with his Yellow Pages and his telephone making an exhaustive tour of New York by wire. The rest of the time he had spent with his TV. His head hurt, his ribs hurt, his arms hurt. He was hard pressed to find anything that didn't hurt. He finally felt justified for having avoided contact sports as a child.

So far his efforts had not been too fruitful in tracking down any useful information about the club on Sixth Avenue. He had tried trade associations, other health clubs, gymnasium suppliers and had even spoken to most of the people in the area who built swimming pools and installed saunas and whirlpools. Nobody he had spoken to, and he had spoken to quite a few people, had ever even heard of, much less done business with, any health club facility that was located in a skyscraper on Sixth Avenue. In one respect Flynn was depressed that he hadn't been able to turn up anything. But, then again, no news was also excellent news. The fact that nobody was able to tell him anything about the place only furthered his suspicions that he was dealing with something very phoney. Next he'd try the laundries. Somebody had to wash their towels. He picked up the phone and punched out a number. He was fast on those buttons and proud of it, too.

"Continental Laundry, good afternoon."

"Oh yeah, hi. I have a question I wanted to ask about your service."

"Yes?"

"Well," said Mark, "I was over as a guest the other

day at that health club in the Northrop Tower and somebody mentioned the name of your company. I'm opening a new facility in Queens myself and I wanted to find out if it was your company that did their laundry, because I was pretty impressed with the service."

"What was the name of the club?"

"Hmmmph," Mark casually laughed, "believe it or not, the name escapes me. I have no memory for names. Well, anyway, it's the only one over there. You know, in the Northrop Tower on Sixth Avenue."

"Well, if you'll hold on a moment I'll check our records and see what I can find."

"Okay, great." There was a muted click as Mark was shifted into the netherworld of Muzak. Being put on hold these days was becoming a genuine assault on one's aesthetic sensibilities. He took a bite out of his sandwich and chewed as fast as he could. He really didn't want to get caught with a mouthful when the woman came back.

"Hello, sir?"

"Eh, yeah," mumbled Mark as he swallowed hard. He coughed half of it back up. "Excuse me... I have a terrible cold. One second." He coughed again and swallowed a sip of Coke. He never understood why, but he always took a bite of something every time he was put on hold. This was not the first time that this same scene had been played. He was a creature of habit he decided. "Hi, I'm back. Sorry."

"That's alright. Now, I've checked our records

thoroughly, but we don't seem to have any health facility accounts in that area. I'm sorry."

"Yeah, that's okay." He ran a dark black line through Continental Laundry in his directory. "Have you any idea who else I might call?"

"Well, you know, sir, Continental Laundry is one of the oldest and best established laundries in New York. We would be most anxious to have one of our sales persons get in touch with you to discuss handling this account ourselves. I'm sure we could do as well, if not better, than whatever it is you saw at this club."

"Oh, excuse me," said Mark, "I never meant to imply that you couldn't. By all means, please have someone call me."

"May I have your name and number, please?"

"Of course. My name is Johnathon... J-o-h-n... right. Shasky... S-h-a-s-k-y... right. And, my number is 832-7225. Right. Thanks very much." Well, that was one down- he looked at the phone book- and about two hundred to go. Whoopee...

III

The Club had been founded in 1956. Many of the first fighters had been soldiers in the Korean Conflict who had felt a sense of loss at the close of the war. Some of them had enjoyed what they were doing enough to want to continue it on what they considered to be a more civilized level, while others felt they simply had not seen enough action and chose to rectify that situation at the Club. In the twenty-five years that the Club had been in existence there had been over five thousand scheduled bouts. An average of four of these per year resulted in a death. Some one hundred men had died in combat at the Club.

At any given time there were generally thirty fighters in the Club's stable. Most lasted between three to five years. Some, of course, lasted much less, while there were a number of fighters who had been at the Club for as long as eight years. Three times a year the Selection Committee met and reviewed the records and condition of all fighters. Those that were no longer considered fit were retired and made free members of the Club for life. Although it was not readily apparent, particularly to the fighters, the odds were very much against them. The ratio of thirty fighters to the approximately four deaths per year seemed to indicate that chances were very slim one would die in combat. In reality, the turnover of five new fighters per year merely covered the four deaths and one retiree that could be statistically expected. If an actual count were made, the surprising truth was that in twenty-five years there had only been a total of 157 fighters connected with the Club. One hundred of these had died in combat. The odds were, therefore, only one in three an individual would survive his career. The members knew this. Perhaps the fighters who had thought about it did also. It was hard to say, as it was never discussed. The accepted interpretation of the figures was that with thirty fighters and two hundred bouts per year, four deaths seemed like pretty good odds.

The Club was the original tenant of the Northrop Tower. Charles Northrop, the president of Northrop Industries which had built the tower, had been one of the founders. The top two floors of the Tower had been designed to accomodate the Club and had long since been a part of the building's plans at the time of construction. It was installed and ready to function long before the building's completion in 1953. There had been five other founding members and it had taken these six men three years of discrete planning and inquiries before they had been able to enlarge their compliment to thirty. When that number had been reached the Club opened and membership increased rapidly thereafter. Through astute judgement and very careful deliberation not one person who they had approached in regards to membership had ever turned down the offer. They all knew each other very well. In 1957 ownership of the two floors occupied by the Club had been turned over to it. Only the members and a few people connected with the building even knew that there was anything up there. The Club was reached through a side entrance in the building. Each member and fighter had two keys. The first opened the street level portal. On the other side of this door an armed guard sat at a desk twenty-four hours a day. He checked all of those who entered for positive identification. The second key operated the elevator which led to the Club itself. The only other way in or out of the Club was through a fire exit which led to the stairs. It could only be opened from the inside in case of an emergency. The Club was on the 63rd and 64th floors.

Twice a year there was a meeting of the Operations Committee and the general membership at which all aspects of the finances and operation of the Club were discussed. It was at these meetings that the normal everyday running of the Club took shape. If some of the members had expressed dissatisfaction with the cooking or the service in the dining room it would be discussed here. If others felt that perhaps one of the meeting rooms should be redecorated then this too would be discussed here. At one meeting a member who had fallen on unexpected bad times broached the subject of resignation. His was the first such request that had ever been made at the Club. It was understood, and in fact agreed in writing, that all members were members for life. Their financial situations were such that the possibility of not being able to continue membership had never been given much serious consideration. After a great deal of discussion it was decided that he would be granted an honorary membership until the time he would be able to resume his financial obligations. The financial status of the Club more than allowed for a generous gesture of this nature. In addition, they were hardly about to let him go. All of the members were agreed that they would sooner support one of their own than see him dissolve his connection with the Club. The Club was so well endowed that there had not been a need to raise per member costs in six years. In fact, they were operating with a substantial surplus.

All of the service personnel who worked at the Club had, with few exceptions, been there since its inception. They were exceedingly well paid, and actually earned more than most doctors or lawyers. They had been as carefully chosen and screened as the members themselves. Except for the fact that they were required to attend to the everyday handling of a large organization's service needs, and that they were paid instead of paying, there was hardly any distinguishing them from the members. They were as committed to the Club as the rest. They were hired for life.

THE KING OF CLUBS

It had now been over a week since Flynn had been beaten up. Although there were areas of his body and psyche that could easily be in a much stronger state, he still felt that it was time for him to hit the streets. So far his inquiries had turned up nothing. For all he had been able to find out there might just as well not be a side entrance to the Northrop Tower. Nobody he had spoken to had ever had anything to do with it or heard anything about it. He began to wonder if perhaps he wasn't barking up the wrong tree. Maybe Linda had been right and the beating he had received hadn't had anything to do with this whole Northrop Tower thing. He decided to take the photos that he had over to Bob Keliman. He had done a number of freelance assignments for him over the years and he and Bob had gotten very friendly. Maybe he could help him figure out who some of these people were and where he should go from this point.

Robert F. Keliman was fifty-six years old and the Chairman of the Board of Sun Publications. He owned three newspapers, eight magazines, numerous subsidiaries and he couldn't stand Mark Flynn. He hadn't liked him since the first time they'd met when Mark was still a boy. But, since he was the son of one of Keliman's oldest friends he had at least felt the obligation to throw him a bone. That had been five years ago and since then Flynn had actually done some very excellent work for him. Keliman considered him to be easily the flippest, most obnoxious person that he knew, but he was a good writer... and that was what counted.

"Hello, Mark," said Keliman. "What happened to you?" he asked as he noticed Flynn's swollen face. "Finally opened that big mouth of yours a little too far?"

"Hey, hey, Bobby, what's happening?" said Flynn as he pulled up a chair. Keliman winced. Flynn was the only man living that called him Bobby. He hated it with a passion. "I've got the license number of the truck that hit me right here. I thought maybe you could help me trace it."

Keliman laughed. The guy might be a pain in the neck but at least he had a sense of humor. Keliman leafed through some papers on his desk while they spoke. He wanted to look busy so Flynn wouldn't be tempted to stay too long.

"So what's up, Mark? What are you working on?"

"Well, Bobby, I'm not exactly sure. First thing I'd like to do is show you some photographs and see if you recognize anybody."

"Okay," said Keliman, adjusting his glasses, "let's see what you've got."

Mark opened up the manila envelope he had brought with him and took out an 8 x 10 glossy black and white photograph. It was a close-up of a middleaged man in a three piece suit. The background was fuzzy and out of focus. Keliman took it from him and studied it for only a second.

"Les McCormick," he said simply and handed it back to Mark. "What are you doing with a photograph of Les McCormick?"

"Who's Les McCormick?" asked Mark.

"Leslie A. McCormick, president of McCormick-Sutter. He manufactures steel. No big news Mark. He's in the Wall Street Journal just about every day."

Mark took out a pen and wrote the name across the bottom of the photo. "Do you know him, Bob?"

"I've met him before," Keliman said as he removed his glasses. He looked Flynn straight in the eyes for the first time since he'd been shown in. "What's the angle, Mark? What's this all about?"

"Well, I think this guy belongs to some kind of a secret organization or something."

"Secret organization? What secret organization?"

"Well, if I knew that, Bobby, it wouldn't be a secret!"

Keliman shifted in his seat. He would try not to lose his patience.

Mark continued. "So anyway, it seems there's this place over on Sixth Avenue that I've been staking out. I don't know what it is, but something very strange is going on over there."

"Well, I can tell you one thing. The only thing strange about Les McCormick is that after playing golf for over thirty-five years he still can't break 100."

"Well, then you can add this to your list... it's because of this photo of McCormick that four very big, very tough guys decided to beat me up."

"Let me see the rest of those photos," said Keliman. Mark passed him the envelope.

After Mark had left, Keliman picked up his private phone and dialed a number. It rang once and was answered by a gruff voice.

"Ostling?"

"Yes."

"This is Robert Keliman."

"Oh hello, Keliman. How are you?"

"I'm okay," he said. "I'm calling to see if we have a problem."

"A problem?" said Ostling.

"One of my freelance writers was just in here with an idea for a new story he's working on."

"Um-hmm."

"He showed me some photographs that he'd taken to see if I recognized any of the people in them."

"Yes."

"The first one that he showed me was of Les McCormick."

"Yes."

"The second was of you."

"Um-hmm."

"They were all taken at the entrance to the Club."

"What's this reporter's name?"

"Well, I'd rather not say just now... for personal reasons."

"Is it Mark Flynn?" asked Ostling.

"Yes," said Keliman, "it is."

"Robert, can you meet me over at the Club around six tonight? We can discuss this matter in more detail then."

"I'll be there." Keliman hung up.

Flynn was feeling a little disappointed as he left the building on Park Avenue and 57th Street. He had really expected Keliman to be a bit more enthusiastic than he had been. Everybody seemed to be treating this entire thing as if it were merely a figment of his imagination. But, the fact of the matter was that certain things could not be denied. Exactly what they were, he wasn't sure... but, certain things could not be denied. He was working with a surfeit of circumstantial, circumstantial evidence. Even if everything that he suspected turned out to be true the best that he would have would be circumstantial evidence that something strange was going on. He still wouldn't know what.

He wandered towards Central Park. It was a beautiful day and he decided to air his wounds and views amongst the trees and flowers of a rapidly approaching New York spring. He bought an ice cream cone and sat on a bench. He watched a street mime try to get out of a glass room. Must have been an occupational hazard. He'd never seen one that hadn't gotten himself locked in a glass room. Damn, there were a lot of chicks out here in the middle of the afternoon. Don't any of them work? He couldn't believe that even though he had been beaten up, was working on one of the great mysteries of his career, was completely embroiled in the heartache of a romantic triangle and wasn't feeling particularly great to boot, his thoughts still never strayed from checking out women for more than twenty minutes. Well, God bless me, he thought.

Let this rest awhile. Rest awhile! He couldn't believe that was what Keliman had said. I'll look into this a bit and see what I can come up with. Then he politely dismissed him as if he were some overanxious third grader looking for a spot on the school paper. Well, the hell with him, thought Flynn. I've gone this far alone, I guess I can continue on alright by myself. Gone this far alone! Where had he gone? The best he had been able to do so far was knock his phone bill up sixty bucks and spend a small fortune on film and prints. He wondered what flicks were playing and started thumbing through a paper someone had left on the bench next to him.

"Hello, Henry," said Keliman as he entered the Board Room. It had been quite some time since he had last been there and he had forgotten how handsome and comfortable it was. His eyes wandered around the room as he surveyed the familiar collection of ancient arms that filled the walls. He had served on the Board from 1971 to 1976.

"Hello, Robert," said Ostling. "Will you have a drink?"

"Just a small scotch, thanks," said Keliman as he sat down at the conference table in the middle of the room. Henry poured him his scotch and joined him at the table.

"Henry," began Keliman abruptly, "did you have Mark Flynn beaten up?"

"Yes," said Ostling.

"What in the world were you thinking of? What are we now... gangsters? That boy might have been hurt."

"I'm sorry, Robert. First of all it was not my decision to make but rather one that was taken by the entire Board. Please bear in mind that this is the first time that we've ever been threatened in this way and, quite frankly, we didn't know exactly what to do."

"So it would seem."

"We had rather hoped that this might persuade him to place his interests elsewhere," said Ostling, "but, this obviously was not the case."

"No, I'm afraid it wasn't. If anything it's only served to increase his curiosity. He's very worked up about this."

Ostling took out a pack of cigarettes and offered one to Keliman. He lit one himself. "Tell me something, Robert, how well do you know this Flynn?"

"Very well."

"Do you think he might be able to fit in here?"

"Fit in?" Keliman laughed. "Are you thinking of making him a member?"

"The thought had crossed my mind."

"Oh, I'm sorry, Henry. You have the wrong man in mind. Flynn was a Vietnam protester. He burned his draft card on the steps of the Boston city hall. No, I'm afraid not."

Ostling took a puff on his cigarette and exhaled slowly. "Can he be bought?" he asked casually.

"Bought?" Keliman looked surprised. "Henry, do you mean to tell me that you don't know whose son this boy is?"

Ostling didn't respond.

"Henry," said Keliman, "didn't you know his father is Paul Flynn?"

"The senator?"

"I'm afraid so."

Ostling pulled the ashtray towards him and put out his cigarette. He looked very taken back by this news.

"You don't suppose he's discussed any of this with his father?" he asked.

"Quite frankly, I don't know," said Keliman, "but, I doubt it. Mark is a very independent young man who would much sooner go to his father with a *fait accompli* rather than a bunch of hopped up suspicions. I would say that it's unlikely."

"Well, we have to know for sure. That's imperative."

"I'm well aware of that. I'll have to see what I can find out."

"This certainly presents a much different problem," said Ostling. He reached for his pack of cigarettes and lit another.

"Yes," said Keliman, "I'm afraid it does."

The weekend for Bill Thomas's family reunion had come and gone. He had actually made a reservation for the flight, but had never picked up the ticket. He had pretty much known all along that he would never go through with it. He didn't even know what it was that had brought the whole idea up in the first place. Besides, it had now been long enough since he'd been hurt for him to slowly begin training again, and he didn't have time to spare running all over the country. He was looking forward to getting back to the Club and starting to loosen up again. He had already started to feel like an old man. For the first time in his life he actually found himself looking forward to that infernal whirlpool.

Lou had told Bill to come over to the Club at around four that afternoon and he would start to put him through the paces again. He showed up at four on the nose, put his things in his locker and went through to the gym. It felt good to be back.

"Hey, Lou. Whattaya say?"

"Well, look who it is back from the dead. Bill Thomas himself."

"Yeah," said Bill. It really did feel great to be back.

"Go on," said Lou, "why don't you get over there and start doing some stretching. I'll be over in a couple of minutes."

"Okay, Lou, sure thing." Bill trotted over to a free space. A couple of the men slapped him on the back as he passed. Bill was smiling from ear to ear.

He slowly began his old regimen and found that he

wasn't as stiff as he'd thought he would be. Fortunately, he had been smart enough to do some light workouts at home during the past week.

After giving Bill about ten minutes alone to warm up, Lou came over to his mat with Cornelius Francis. They watched quietly as Bill finished the exercise he was working on.

"Bill," said Lou, "I want you to meet Cornelius Francis."

Bill held out his hand to the young fighter. "Hi," he said, "I caught your match the other night. You did a fine job."

"Thank you very much, Mr. Thomas. I see you fighting many times and I think you are the greatest." Cornelius smiled broadly, displaying a big gap between his two front teeth. He was obviously very pleased to be talking with Bill.

Bill nodded. "Thanks," he said.

"I told you the other day," said Lou, "that I was kind of hoping I could get the two of you together for some workouts. Now that you're back we can probably start you off doing some light work. I really think Cornelius here can learn a lot from you, Bill. I want to move him into weapons as soon as possible."

"That's fine with me," said Bill. "It'd be my pleasure."

"Okay then," said Lou, "we'll just leave you to it. I'll start the two of you off together at the beginning of next week."

"Fine," said Bill as he went back to his stretching.

"Thank you very much, Mr. Thomas," said Cornelius

in his light, rich accent. "I appreciate your kindness."

Paul Flynn, Mark's father, was a character. He had been in the Senate for the past twenty years, since Mark was a child, and was considered by the majority of his peers as the original bleeding heart liberal. At the time when most of Mark's friends were rebelling against everything their parents stood for, Mark had only been able to jump on the bandwagon. His father already had first dibs on all of the good causes and Mark's only choice was capitulation or fascism. Mark chose to capitulate with a vengeance. He joined the Students for a Democratic Society, organized rallies and had both major and minor flirtations with the likes of the Yippies and the Weathermen. He was even at the Chicago Democratic Convention. Unfortunately, he hadn't been able to get arrested. He'd certainly tried hard enough, though.

Senator Flynn was crazy about Mark. In the Sixties he had watched with pride as his son helped to tear down the bastians of corruption. He watched now, also with pride, as Mark's career in investigative reporting semi-burdgeoned. He followed everything that Mark worked on closely and secretly wished he'd just go into some nice, simple business. One firebrand in the family was quite enough. Unfortunately, it was a transition in his career that Mark would have to make on his own. Anything that he might suggest in relation to this particular question would only serve to convince Mark that what he was doing was right. He'd have to grow bored with it himself. Mark, the Senator was convinced, was one of those people who was excessively cause-oriented. He knew where all the major fights were and he knew where the battlelines were drawn. But, he never seemed to firmly grasp the nature, the essence, of the true debate. Many people could (and did) say the same thing about the Senator. Well, as far as he was concerned, they simply didn't know what the hell they were talking about. Flynn was about 57 years old, distinguished, as senators will often be, and just "hip" enough to foster his much deserved and treasured image. He was so loved by his constituents that it was said it would take either an act of Congress or an act of God to get him out of the Senate. As far as Paul Flynn was concerned, he had a hell of a lot more to fear from Congress.

He and his wife lived in a large, five bedroom house in Chevy Chase. It was here that Mark had lived from the time he was ten until he left for college. He had grown up here with his two sisters who were now both married to lawyers. Shaunie and Sheryl both lived in Washington, D.C. not too far from the center of the "action" as their father liked to call it. Allan Weinstein and Nicky Ryan, Mark's two brothers-in-law, both worked for the federal government. One of the Senator's most famous quotations was this: "Nepotism ... my ass!"

John Shasky's family lived in the house catty-corner

to the Flynn's. John's father was also connected with the government. He had originally started out as an attorney but, since coming to Washington in the fifties, had been bounced around from one executive post to another in agency after agency. He was a real bureaucrat and proud of it. He liked to boast that he had been, during the course of his career, to at least one party in every embassy in town.

When John had first asked him if he wanted to go home for the weekend Mark's response had been an emphatic No! But, the more he thought about it the more it seemed like it might be a nice way to cop a couple of days vacation and get a change of scenery to boot. He hadn't seen his parents in over two months and, despite the aggravation, he realized he wouldn't mind seeing his sisters and all the nieces, nephews and husbands that went with them.

Flynn and Shasky met at Penn Station about fifteen minutes before their train was due to leave. That meant they should be en route in about a half an hour or so. They bought metroliner tickets in the coach section. If the train wasn't crowded they'd try and sneak up into the club car later.

Before going down to the track they stopped at a newstand and Flynn bought a copy of *Penthouse*. John bought a copy of *Blue Boy*. Mark made a mental note to hold his *Penthouse* up high for all to see whenever John felt tempted to peruse his *Blue Boy*. Guilt by association. Flynn wondered if perhaps his homosexual fears didn't mean that he was really a closet queen. He'd have to pick up a copy of Kinsey or something when he got home.

"Hey, John," said Mark after they had gotten arranged in their seats. "Did you ever tell your parents that you were gay?"

"Yeah right!" laughed John. "What're you kidding?"

"But, what about gay pride and all that shit?" said Mark.

"Oh come on, Mark... whattaya think I wanna do, give my mother a heart attack?"

"Why? Don't you think they could handle it?"

"Not a chance."

"How about if you were going out with a doctor?"

"That's very funny, Mark. Really it is. I get a kick out of it every time I hear it."

"Well," said Flynn, "I'm a funny guy... what can I say?"

"Really, Flynn, I don't know how you stand yourself... you're such an incredible pain!"

"Because, my dear Johnathon, I have many redeeming qualities. I feel that that which I have to offer the world far outweighs my many defects."

"I think you need a new scale."

"Thank you."

"Thank you." They bowed towards each other.

John took his magazine out of his shoulder bag and settled back in his seat. Flynn took out his *Penthouse* and held it over his head.

"Alright... cut it out, willya," said John. "Enough's

enough!"

"Excuse me," said Flynn sarcastically. "I was only trying to defend my reputation." He opened his magazine to the centerfold and ogled it appreciatively. He angled the magazine towards John and waited, set to pounce, for him to try and take a peek. John opened his magazine to a nice full color reproduction and pointed it towards Flynn. Mark did not have John's self control, or at least lack of interest. He stared.

"Umm," purred John in his most effeminate voice. "I see you like big ones, too..."

Flynn blushed and went back to his own magazine. He was sure he'd pick up that Kinsey now. They were traveling twenty minutes before either of them next spoke. Flynn had gotten tired of his magazine and was staring absently out the window. The scenery was anything but spectacular.

"Hey, by the way, what's happening with all your women?" asked John.

"Seriously?" said Mark.

"Yeah, seriously."

"Well, between you and me, it's getting to be a bit of a drag."

"How do you mean?"

"Well, at first it was a lot of fun, but now all the lying and scheming is starting to get me down. When I'm with Linda I'm constantly afraid that Nina's going to call, and when I'm with Nina I'm constantly afraid that Linda's going to call. Then, all that crap about having to figure out where I'm going to tell Linda I was when I was with Nina. It's a drag."

"How about all that sex, though..." said John nudging Mark slyly in the side.

"Ah, same thing. At first it was really great, but now I just can't handle it. I feel like some kind of stud service... always on call. Me and Seattle Slew. It's gotten to the point where the most fun I have is staying home and watching TV."

"That's too bad..."

Mark shrugged.

"So what are you going to do about it?" asked John.

"To tell you the truth I haven't the slightest idea. I mean, I'm crazy about both of them, but not in the same way. I guess I'm just going to have to let it ride for awhile. See what happens."

"I wouldn't let it go too long."

"Don't worry... I can't. I'm about ready to bust as it is."

"So what's this Nina do anyway?"

"Believe it or not she's got a PhD and does cancer research," said Mark with pride. He felt it was a good reflection on himself.

"Really?" said John. He was impressed.

"Yeah... she's a genuine bright cookie."

"So what in the world does she talk to you about?"

"Nothing... I can't keep up with her. She's just into my looks."

"She's into your looks?" said John in disbelief.

"Yeah," said Mark.

"Jesus," said John, "it must be tough for her to do all that research stuff being blind and all."

"Thank you," said Mark.

"Thank you," said John. They bowed to each other again.

"So how about you," asked Mark, "how's your friend Bill?"

"I wouldn't know. I haven't seen him since that night we had dinner together."

"How come?"

"Well, I guess we had a fight or something."

"You guess... don't you know?"

"Well, he just got very pissed at me and we haven't spoken to each other since. I think he probably went back to Chicago."

"What'd he get so pissed about?"

"Coincidentally enough," said John accusingly, "it was about you."

"Me?" exclaimed Flynn. "What have I got to do with the comings and goings of the West Village underworld?"

"Nothing, as far as I know... yet. He just got real pissed when I told him that you wanted to keep looking into that dumb club of his."

"No kidding?" Flynn's professional curiosity stood up and took notice.

"He said creeps like you should mind their own business. Then he said something about the size of your nose and how you shouldn't keep sticking it in other people's lives."

"He said I should mind my own business?"

"That he did."

"And you had dinner with him the night before I was beaten up," said Flynn. He didn't need a calculator to put two and two together. He could do it in his head and come up with five everytime.

"Yeah," said John. "He was the one in the bandages leaning on a cane."

"Nobody likes a crippled bully, you know."

"Yeah!" cheered John.

"Yeah!" echoed Flynn. "I shoulda taken that cane away from him! See how he likes it!"

"You macho guy, you... wanna take a look at this?" He threw his *Blue Boy* in Mark's lap.

"By the way," said Mark, "what'd you do with that whip I loaned you?"

Most of the members' wives knew that their husbands belonged to some sort of club, the exact nature of which was never revealed. It had always been presented to them as a retreat for men only. The rationale was that men of their stature, dealing with the kinds of pressures that they dealt with, needed to have a place to get away to that was not known to any outside people. It was like a hideaway apart from the daily fray, where they could go to sauna, exercise and have some dinner with friends. None of the wives knew who any of the other members were and they were all sworn to absolute secrecy about the Club's existence. It was like a game for them. None of them knew where the Club was located and none of them cared. It was a privelege the men did not abuse, rarely going to the Club more than once or twice a week. In the beginning the rules did not allow anything to be mentioned to the wives, but this made things terribly awkward as they would always want an explanation as to the whereabouts of their husbands. It was finally decided to tell them that they were members of a fraternity of sorts and to emphasize that secrecy was its most important element. The women treated it like they would the Elks or the Masons. It was like the secret societies they remembered from college. And, after all, were men anything more than large boys anyway? It represented no threat or imposition on their lives so they were never prompted to question it. For a wife to discuss it or mention it to anyone meant instant expulsion for the member, they were told, and they were, to a one, most willing to accept this explanation.

"Well," said Dick Alston, "as far as I'm concerned the time to start worrying is when East and West Germany reunify."

"Why is that?" asked Malcolm Anderson.

"It's the march-every-thirty-years-or-die syndrome," said Dick. "In the thirty some odd years since the war ended West Germany has managed to become one of the strongest industrial powers in the world. Some way to lose a war. If they ever got back together again, it would only be a matter of time before somebody over there decided that it would be better for all concerned if they simply took over the world. For our own good, you understand."

Malcolm laughed. "I don't know what you're so worried about... you've got the prerequisite blonde hair and blue eyes."

"It's not me I'm worried about," said Dick gravely, "it's Murray that has me concerned." He winked at Malcolm.

"What?" said Murray. "Send this boy to summer camp? Jawohl, mein herr!" He gave his friends a straight arm salute. They all laughed.

"Well, if there were another war," said Malcolm, "and we were lucky enough for it to start between Russia and China that would certainly help keep them apart."

"Well, all I know," said Dick, "is that they're awfully good customers."

"Not half so good as we are to them," said Murray.

"I wouldn't know," said Malcolm. "I only sell to them. I haven't bought a thing of theirs in ten years." He smiled. He figured he was pretty sharp.

The waiter brought the check and a pencil to the table. Murray grabbed it over the protests of his dinner companions. "No, no," he said, "this one's on me."

"Jack," said Dick to the waiter, "could we get some more coffee too when you get a chance."

"Certainly, Mr. Alston."

Murray signed his name and handed the check back to the waiter. "By the way," he said, "did either of you speak to Ostling?"

They both nodded.

"Did he tell you about this Flynn complication?" He could tell from the looks on their faces that they'd heard.

"I know Paul Flynn," said Malcolm.

"Is that right?"

"We've met quite a few times at dinner parties. Very strange fellow."

"Would you say you carry any weight with him?" asked Murray.

Malcolm shrugged. "I doubt it. He's a very righteous man. Self-inflated. He doesn't like to think anyone's able to influence him."

"Like father like son," said Dick.

"Um-hmm," said Murray. He put a teaspoon of sugar in his coffee and stirred it. "If the need should arise, is there anything we could get on him?" he asked Malcolm.

Malcolm shrugged again. "It's not altogether impossible." Murray and Dick both looked up. "But, I honestly don't know how he'd react to that kind of pressure."

"Well," said Murray, "maybe you could look into it a bit and let us know."

Malcolm nodded.

"Tell me something, Mr. Thomas," asked Cornelius Francis in his sing-song accent, "what do you think happens to a man when he dies?"

Bill and Cornelius were in the locker room changing into their street clothes. They had just finished their first workout together. It had gone well. Cornelius was a fast learner and the two men seemed to work well together.

"Well, first of all, please don't call me Mr. Thomas... my name is Bill." Cornelius smiled. "And, secondly, you've got the wrong guy for that question."

"Why is that, sir?" asked Cornelius.

"Because I haven't got any of the answers. Sometimes I think I do, but most of the time I'm just as confused as you."

"Do you think there is a God?"

"Oh, I guess so... I don't know. Sometimes I think that when you die, that's it. No more. And, sometimes I think that there's a God and a heaven and all that stuff."

"What do you think about reincarnation?" asked Cornelius.

"Reincarnation?" laughed Bill. "You got me there. I don't know anything about that stuff. I once knew this girl that thought she used to be a tree. She told me I had what they call an old soul. Then I fucked her."

Cornelius giggled. He was a really nice kid, thought Bill.

"How many men have you killed when you are fighting?" asked Cornelius. The question took Bill by surprise. He didn't really want to talk about it.

"I don't know," he said. "I never really counted."

"Is it that many?" said Cornelius. Bill detected a note of awe in his voice. He didn't like that.

"No, it's not that many. It's only two," said Bill. This whole conversation was starting to make him uncomfortable.

"How did you feel when you did it?"

Well, figured Bill, I guess he has a right to know this kind of stuff if he's going to have to fight. "It didn't feel so great. I was friendly with both these guys and I'd just as soon it hadn't happened, y'know."

Cornelius was silent for a moment. He was trying to formulate his next question.

"But, you know," said Bill, "you gotta remember that everybody knows what they're up against here, and they all have to take responsibility for themselves."

"Do you think, Mr. Thomas, that what we do here is right?"

"Right?"

"I mean is what happens here alright with God?"

"With God? Well, I don't know if it's alright with God, but it's alright with me."

"You don't think we are damned for what we do?"

Bill gave him a quick pat on the shoulder and smiled. "Take it from me, Cornelius, you don't have to worry about that. We're not damned." He picked up his bag and headed for the door. "Take it easy, Cornelius, I'll see you later. And, don't think too hard about that kind of stuff. You gotta just play it like you see it."

"Hi," said Mark, "is Bob Keliman there?"

"Who's calling please?"

"Mark Flynn."

"One moment, Mr. Flynn, I'll see if he's in."

A new secretary, thought Mark. The other one had known his name so he never got the haughty tone that he'd just gotten from this one. Well at least they didn't have Muzak on the line. You had to be thankful for the little things.

"Hello, Mark?" said Keliman.

"Hey, Bobby, how are you?"

"Fine, fine... where are you? I've tried to reach you a couple of times." He had actually tried about thirty times.

"I'm down in Washington... I decided to come down and see my folks for a few days."

"Oh, that's great... please send them my regards." Keliman didn't like hearing Mark was in Washington. Too close to his father.

"I will, don't worry. So, what's the story? Did you turn up anything yet, or what?"

"Well, as a matter of fact, I have."

"No kidding! What'd you come up with?"

"First let me tell you that it's not as spectacular as you thought."

"No?"

"I'm afraid not. And, secondly I have to emphasize that this must be kept in strict confidence between ourselves. It's a favor that was asked of me, and I gave my word. Is that okay with you?"

Mark crossed his fingers. "Sure, Bobby, anything you say."

"Mark, have you discussed any of this with your father?"

"No, not yet."

"Well, that's another part of this. I would prefer it if you didn't. This will have to be between you and I."

"If that's what you want... sounds pretty serious."

"Please don't let my tone fool you... it's not that serious at all."

"Well then lay it on me." Flynn loved to use old hippy phrases on middleaged people. It made them feel so with it just to have understood him.

"Well, this is what I've found out... it seems that what you've stumbled onto is a private club that a bunch of wealthy snobs set up to enjoy their money and to avoid contact with the have nots."

"Go on," said Mark.

"Well, they've been around there for about ten or fifteen years and believe it or not you're the first outsider to have ever gotten wind of the place."

"So why all the secrecy?"

"These guys really treasure their privacy. They have a nice set-up there with a gym and saunas and all and they don't want anybody to know anything about it. Even their wives don't know where it is."

"How liberated."

"Yeah, I suppose it is a little ridiculous. They're like a bunch of fraternity jocks or something, but the people involved are very influential and that's the way they want it."

"So what's this stuff about it being just between you and me?"

"Well, two of the men who belong happen to be close friends of mine and people I owe some favors to. They asked me to personally see that word of this club doesn't get out, and quite frankly I can't see what harm it would do to let the whole thing lie. Let them have their fun, you know what I mean?"

"So if all of this is so innocent, why did they have me beat up?" asked Mark.

"From everything I've been able to determine, they didn't."

"Bullshit! If they didn't, who did?"

"Mark, I haven't the slightest idea. But, between you and I you have a very loose mouth and you've never seemed to care very much where you let it flap. I could probably come up with a dozen people who would like to have done it, if they'd only thought of it."

"Yeah, well thanks for the good news, Bobby. I sure appreciate it."

"That's okay... I guess we'll just call this one closed then."

"Yeah," said Flynn, "I guess so."

"Listen," said Keliman, "why don't you give me a ring when you get back to town. We'll get together for some lunch. I might have a couple of things coming up for you, too."

"Oh say, that'll be great, Bobby. I'll see you then."

"So long, kid."

"Yeah, so long." Bullshit! thought Mark as he slammed down the phone. Who the hell did they think they were kidding?"

Linda Hoskins stood in the shower of her apartment on East 76th Street. She lived in a doorman building with an automatic elevator and L-shaped living rooms. She was listed in the phone book as L. Hoskins to avoid letting people who made obscene phone calls know that a single girl lived at that number. People who make obscene phone calls, however, always look for numbers where the name is only listed with the first initial. They know this invariably indicates a single girl. Linda Hoskins was a New York City single girl. She had moved to Manhattan six years ago after dropping out of college ten credits short of a degree. She was from Michigan.

Linda had just bought one of those massager heads for her shower and she had gotten the building's handyman to install it for her. Now, even though she had as yet not been able to figure out what benefits were to be derived from her new investment, she felt an obligation to shower for as long as possible each day. In this way she hoped to fool her subconscious into believing that she really loved her new shower head and that it had been a great buy. In reality she wasn't able to tell the difference between it and the old one. Well, perhaps it wasn't the shower head's fault, she thought. I probably just don't have enough water pressure to make the stupid thing work right, that's all.

For the past two weeks Linda had not been feeling well. Oh, she was alright physically. It was spiritually that she hurt. She wasn't sure why, perhaps it was just woman's intuition, but she knew there was something wrong in her relationship with Mark. She could sense it. She could hear it in his voice when they spoke on the phone and she could see it in his face when they were together. The terrible sense of malaise that this situation was causing her was affecting her life dramatically. She couldn't work, she couldn't sleep and she couldn't eat. These, she was sure, were not good signs. Yesterday, she had had to leave the office early and go for a walk. She felt like she was going to throw up. Linda was a writer also. She worked for a large advertising agency in midtown and earned a very comfortable living as a copywriter. She had started at the same agency when she first moved to New York. Amazingly enough everything had worked out perfectly and after six years she was still with the same firm. Promotions had been regular and salary increases had been generous. She loved her work. She also enjoyed a reputation as one of the fastest and most reliable copywriters in the business.

Being a writer herself was perhaps the major reason

that she was not able to comprehend Mark and his work. He sat home all day, watched TV and ate. This he called work. He picked up on any stupid idea that occurred to him and followed it through to its inevitable death, as most of them never amounted to anything. In the entire time she had been seeing him, two and a half years, he had had three stories published for a gross capital gain of approximately $8,000. He had probably spent four times that amount just keeping himself alive and healthy. And yet, he was pleased with his progress and insisted that someday he would win a Pulitzer Prize and be beating magazines and newspapers off with a stick. This, as far as she was concerned, constituted the essence of incompatibility. All they had to do was tell her the name of a product and the mood they wanted to convey and she could throw the finished copy back at them in fifteen minutes. Mark, on the other hand, needed all the elements to be right. If he didn't feel it he didn't write it. That, according to Linda, was his major problem. Discipline. What he needed was a good spanking.

As the water fell on her body Linda ran her hands up her arms. She was trying to "feel" herself and her body as a part of the Universe. Mark had told her that it was possible to "feel" oneself in relation to the Universe and all other things. God, she did not understand him. It was amazing. Half the time she didn't even know what the hell he was talking about. She didn't need to "feel" herself. She already understood herself perfectly. She was Linda Hoskins, 28. A New

Yorker and a writer. A human being. She was sure he must be seeing another woman. There was really no other explanation. For all of her adult life she had reveled in her ability to stay single, free and creative. To make it on her own in what had always been a man's world. And now, at 28, she found herself realizing how much she wanted the stability of a long term relationship. Somebody to grow old with and have children with. She couldn't believe she'd wasted two and a half years of precious time on Mark Flynn.

Mark was stoned to the bone. He had dropped a lude and he had, at this point, no control over what he did. He could hardly see straight and he loved it. Total release from the real world. It was four in the morning and he was dancing all over his parent's living room trying, without much success, not to knock anything other than himself over. Who cared about Pulitzer Prizes and world reknown? Who cared about applause from the masses? All he cared about was the buzz. And it was a good one, too. He had lost all sense of time and space. He was God knows where and happy to be there. It was amazing, he reflected as he stood back up, how the pretenses and facades of everyday life had nothing to do with this level of experience. He felt free and ready to go. If he never came back it wouldn't bother him in the least. He was basking in the luxury of total indifference. So what if

99.999% of the people in the world didn't know their asses from their elbows? If they didn't like it they could lump it. He felt great.

Quaaludes, being essentially a sleeping pill as well as an hypnotic, can very often impose their prescribed effects on the reluctant merrymaker. Mark never made it to bed. He fell asleep on the couch in the den watching "Give Us This Day".

"Mark," said a voice that sounded like cotton. Or was it that his brain felt like cotton? He wasn't sure. Didn't make much difference.

"Mark," came that voice again. Somebody was shaking him. With an almost superhuman effort Mark managed to open his eyes. He felt like he had been asleep for only two minutes, but as his father was standing in front of him in a suit and tie it had to be at least 8:30. He knew he was still stoned, but he should at least have more control over himself now that he had slept a bit... he hoped. He sat up slowly, testing his condition as he went. "Hi, Dad," he said, "what's happening?"

"Mark," said the Senator, "what are you doing here?"

"Nothing, Dad, I was just watching a late night movie and I guess I fell asleep."

"I guess so," said the Senator. He walked over to the television and turned it off. "Do you want some breakfast?"

Breakfast? Mark hadn't even had his before bedtime

snack yet. "Sure, Dad, sounds good."

They went into the kitchen together. Mark with some difficulty. He could always put it off to being groggy after a poor night's sleep on the couch.

Rebecca Walker, their cook and housekeeper for the past eighteen years, was scrambling some eggs and making some bacon. "Mark," she scolded, "what you mean sleeping in the den like that?"

During the years that Mark had been in college Rebecca had been one of his major embarrassments. Here he was one of the spearheads (as far as he was concerned) of the civil rights movement, and every time he brought one of his black friends home he had had to contend with antebellum Rebecca doing her Butterfly McQueen impression. She couldn't have been more stereotyped if she tried. It turned out much later on that the problem was more in his head than hers. When he finally had found the courage to broach the subject it became apparent that Rebecca was quite dedicated to what she did. She insisted that she felt neither degraded nor demeaned in her position, but rather that she was treated with respect and took a great deal of pride in running a household and having been a second mother to a family of five. Mark, only slightly convinced, still insisted that she join the Household Technicians of America and that everybody in the house expunge the word "maid" from their vocabularies. She humored him and joined. Now she was an officer in her local chapter and Mark was finally learning to deal with his guilt.

"Hey," said Mark, "what's the big deal? You'd think I killed somebody or something."

"With all the noise I heard comin' out of there las' night, I'm jus' surprised you didn't kill yourself!"

The Senator looked up quizzically from the paper he was just opening. Mark let the comment slide and Rebecca covered for him.

"Senator, how many slices of bacon do you want?"

"Oh, two will be fine, thank you, Rebecca." He started to turn back to Mark, but Mark beat him to the punch.

"So tell me, Dad, what's new on the Hill?"

"Not too much, son... just the things you read about in the paper. That is if you read the paper."

Oh no, thought Mark, not this again. "Dad, I keep telling you I read the paper every day."

"Well, I don't see why you don't have the *Times* delivered. That way you'd have it right there in the morning."

"Because," Mark began patiently, "I've told you a thousand times... I live on the top floor of my building and the best I could get them to do would be to leave it outside the front door. That means every morning when I got up I'd have to run down five flights of stairs and back up again. It's just not worth it to me. I'd rather wait to pick it up when I go out."

"I'd be willing to pay for it," said the Senator.

"Dad," said Mark, "that's not the point! I can pay for it myself. I just don't want to run down the stairs every morning... that's all."

"Here," said the Senator, handing Mark a coupon he had just ripped out of his copy of the *Times*. "Why don't you fill this out and we'll send it in."

"You know you're going to drive me crazy!" Well, one thing was for sure. He wasn't stoned anymore. His father was better than coffee. And only half the caffeine, too.

"Are you working on anything, Mark?" asked his father as Rebecca brought their food over. She winked at Mark. He gave her a knowing smile. They had both participated in the same scene dozens of times.

"Yeah, as a matter of fact I am," said Mark. "It's kind of interesting, too."

"Tell me about it." The Senator turned to the next page in his paper. Mark couldn't even see his face.

"Well, it seems I've uncovered this secret club that a bunch of very rich guys belong to."

"Um-hmm."

"Yeah, I've been staking out the place and taking photos and they're getting pretty upset."

"Who belongs to this club?"

"Uh, Henry Ostling for one."

"Ostling from A.R.L.?"

"Yeah," said Mark, "that's the guy."

"Who else?"

"Leslie McCormick."

"McCormick-Sutter."

"Yeah."

"Where is this club?"

"On Sixth Avenue in the Northrop Tower."

"Well," said the Senator, "nobody ever invited me there."

"Gee, Dad, I hope your feelings aren't too bruised, but that's not quite the point. It's a *secret* club. Nobody except the members are supposed to know it exists."

"Sounds pretty childish."

"Not to me."

"I fail to see what great interest a story like this would have."

"Well, I think something fishy is going on over there."

"And what makes you think that?"

"Well, when I started getting close, they had four guys beat me up."

"You were beaten up?"

"Yes."

"That's what comes from living in that ridiculous neighborhood of yours. Why can't you find an apartment uptown in a decent area?" The Senator was getting himself upset.

"Dad, I said that these guys had me beat up."

"And how, may I ask, do you know that it was their doing? Was Ostling with them?" The Senator laughed.

"No," said Mark. He was getting annoyed. "Ostling wasn't with them... it just so happens that there isn't anyone else that would want to do something like that. That's how I know!"

"Didn't you tell me you were having women trouble?"

"Yes."

"And that this other woman had a boyfriend."

"Yeah," said Mark cautiously. He knew where this was going to lead. He didn't want to hear it, because it made sense. He hated when his father knew better than he.

"Isn't it possible," asked the Senator, "that this other man was subtly trying to tell you to leave his girlfriend alone?"

"Yeah," conceded Mark grudgingly. He was beginning to wonder why nobody was having any difficulty coming up with suggestions of people who would like to have beaten him up. He'd always thought of himself as likable. "I suppose it is, but I just don't think that's the case."

"Um-hmm," said the Senator as he picked up his paper again. "Did you get hurt?"

"No, it wasn't anything serious."

"Move uptown."

"Alright, alright..."

"And order that paper."

"Oh, for Christ's sake!"

Rebecca smiled. Mark was her boy who wouldn't grow up. She didn't mind though. She loved him that way.

"No, no," shouted Bill, "Higher, Cornelius. If you try to block an axe blow that low you'll lose your God-damn balls!"

Cornelius looked down sheepishly. "I'm sorry, Mr. Thomas."

"Well, don't be so sorry, just do it right," said Bill. He raised his axe and came at Cornelius again. As Bill swung his axe overhead at the younger fighter Cornelius caught the blow on his own axe just short of his head. "That's the idea," said Bill. "Now you've got it."

"Thank you, sir," he grinned.

"Hey, Francis," yelled Jeff Simpson from across the room. "You'd better watch out for Thomas when he starts talking about blows and balls, you know what I mean?" Simpson was boxing with another fighter, Carlos Diaz. Diaz didn't laugh as loudly as Simpson would have liked him to. He'd fought with Thomas before and lost. He followed the prudent course. "Hey, Simpson," he said, "c'mon, let's go, I gotta get home, y'know."

"Hold your water, Diaz... hey, Thomas," he yelled, "whattaya think, you like that black meat, or what?"

Bill put down his axe, walked over to the ring and vaulted the ropes. "Hey, Simpson, what's your problem? I mean what'd I ever do to you, huh?"

"You, you dumb faggot," said Simpson sticking his face right in Bill's, "offend my delicate sensibilities." He laughed at his own wit and turned towards Diaz for for a little peer approval. Bill hauled off and hit him in the side of the face as hard as he could. He knew there'd be hell to pay later, but for the moment it was worth it. Simpson fell like a rock. Bill left the ring and went back to his mat. He picked up his axe again. "Now," he said, "if a guy comes at you with a side-swipe..."

"Hey, Bill..."

"Oh hi, Lou, how you doing? I was just showing Cornelius here about..."

"That was a hell of a nice punch," said Lou.

"Thanks," said Bill modestly.

"It's gonna cost you two grand."

"Yeah? So how do I make out the check?"

They all laughed. Simpson had it coming.

It was six o'clock when the Board members and Robert Keliman broke up what must have been their fifth or sixth meeting devoted exclusively to the subject of Mark Flynn. They were all getting a little tired of the problem that this overly zealous reporter had created for them and were therefore quite glad to hear Keliman's report that Flynn had believed his story. They were exceptionally pleased to learn that Flynn had also said that he hadn't and wouldn't mention anything to his father. They had decided that it would be an excellent idea to invite Mark up to the Club on a night when there was no scheduled fight and show him around. The more they thought about it the more convinced they were that there was no reason the Club could not pass for exactly what its cover story implied it was. They'd give him some dinner and swear him to secrecy. Let him feel privileged knowing he was the only non-member to have ever been inside. After all, they reasoned, he already knew exactly where the place was. All a move like this could serve to do would be to reinforce their story in Mark's mind. Show him that they had nothing to hide. It would be a goodwill gesture.

IV

Mark took a sip of wine, wiped his mouth and leaned back in his chair. He was about to let out a huge belch but decided to exercise some discretion. This was, he was sure, indicative of what he saw as his ever-increasing maturity. Well, one thing was for sure. Whatever else it was that was going on up here, they sure put on a hell of a feed.

Mark was seated at a table in the middle of a very large, elegant dining room which he found surprisingly empty. If he belonged to a club that served such good food he was sure he'd make a point of dining there often.

"Well, Mark," asked Henry Ostling, "how can we tell the chef you rate his efforts?"

"How about by phone," said Mark. Ostling laughed politely. "No, I'm just kidding, Mr. Ostling... it was excellent, really excellent."

The other men at the table smiled their appreciation. They were Murray Weissman, Dick Alston and Malcolm Anderson.

"In fact," said Mark, "the food and service are so good, I was just wondering why there were no other people eating here."

"Mondays are always slow around here, Mr. Flynn," said Malcolm. "Most of the members are still resting up from whatever excesses they've allowed themselves over the weekend." The truth was the Club was closed on Mondays.

"And also," said Ostling, "to be perfectly frank, Mark, the main element of our club's makeup is its secrecy... I'm afraid most of our members simply did not wish to risk exposing themselves to you."

"I'm harmless enough," said Mark.

"Well," laughed Ostling, "I don't know about that. For awhile there you put yourself in a position that could have ended everything that we've been able to put together here."

"Isn't that going a bit far?" asked Mark.

"Not at all, Mr. Flynn," said Murray Weissman. "There are hundreds of clubs in and around New York. The only thing that makes us different from the rest of them is that we are able to offer total privacy to our members."

"For men in responsible positions," said Anderson, "that's a terribly desirable thing."

"Surely you can understand, Mark," said Ostling, "what a refreshing and revitalizing element in a man's life it is to have a place to go where he can completely relax. A place where he doesn't have to worry about phone calls from the office or home. A place that's like taking a short vacation from the world every time he walks through the door."

"Well sure," said Mark, "I can understand that. It sure as hell beats the YMCA."

"Exactly," said Ostling.

"So, then it shouldn't be so hard to understand what a problem you presented for us when we first began to fear you were going to write an article about our place," said Murray. "Without our unique quality of secrecy we might as well close up shop. Most of our members have to go out of their way to come here. They have other affiliations that, without our uniqueness, would quickly make themselves felt. Some would join university clubs and others would join country clubs. Without the element of privacy there would be no need for this club to exist. I for one, and I know I speak for all of us, would resign immediately."

"Well, I can appreciate that," said Mark, "but I still fail to see why you had to have me beaten up." There was a long silence at the table. Mark was sure they were stewing on that one.

"Beaten up?" said Ostling. "What are you talking about?"

"I was saying that I'm not all that irrational that I can't listen to reason. There was really no need to set that bunch of thugs on me."

"Mr. Flynn," said Dick Alston, "I'm amazed to hear this. I'm sure we're all terribly upset that something adverse might have happened to you, but I would think that just by looking at the men at this table you should be able to dismiss the possibility of our having been the cause out of hand. We are hardly the type of men to run around having people beaten up. Not even our precious privacy is important enough to warrant that."

Very lofty, very convincing, thought Mark, but he couldn't help remembering some of the things that Henry Ostling had said at the time he had interviewed him. If these men were his cohorts he was sure that there was very little that they too wouldn't do to protect that which they felt was theirs to protect. He had already checked with Nina to see whether or not his father's idea might hold water, and she assured him that it didn't. Steve, her boyfriend, knew nothing about her seeing Mark. He was a lawyer and had only recently started a new job. They didn't live together and he was swamped with work. For the past two months he had hardly even taken notice of her comings and goings. Say what they might, Mark was sure that he was having dinner with the men who, by proxy, had beaten him up.

"Well," said Mark diplomatically, "I've never been one to deny that I can be wrong. Plus, as is pointed out to me more and more often these days, there are many people who don't seem to wish me the best."

"Well, I certainly hope you weren't hurt," said Alston.

"No, it wasn't anything too serious."

"Well, thank heaven for that."

"Gentlemen," said Ostling, "may I suggest that we take our guest on a tour of the facilities?"

"Excellent idea," said Murray.

A layout and a half, thought Mark, as his dinner companions led him from room to room. As if he hadn't been impressed enough right from the start. First the private entrance and elevator off the street, then a scotch in the oak panelled bar and finally dinner in literally one of the nicest dining rooms he had ever seen. Now they were taking him through the locker room and gymnasium. They showed him the Board Room with its impressive collection of weapons and they showed him the rooms where members could spend the night. Everything about the place was first class and Mark found himself wondering if writing was really what he wanted to do. Burger King was great and all, but...

By the time the evening was over, Mark had to admit, even though he was sure they weren't telling him everything, that there didn't seem to be much for these men to hide. He wasn't crazy about them or their politics or, for the most part, their businesses. But, try as hard as he could, and he had tried very hard, he didn't seem to be able to pin a thing on them. The fact of the matter was, he was sure, that he was making a mountain out of a molehill, which was what everybody told him he was always doing. He guessed it was another sign of his fast approaching maturity that he was willing to admit it. He wasn't so sure though that he agreed with Weissman's contention that the Club would fold if word of its existence were ever to leak out. Already he was formulating in his mind the concept for a story that would mention no names or addresses. The secret club that remains a secret. He was sure that he could sell something like that with no problem. It wouldn't be anything compared to what he had originally hoped to write, but he might be able to at least salvage something from all this. He was sure that these big shots couldn't have any objections to something as innocent as that. Just in case, though, he'd keep his big mouth shut this time.

Alex Nogrady was getting old. He knew it. He could feel it. After his last fight when he had beaten Tom Fenn it had taken him almost twice as long to recuperate as usual. He was 39 years old and had been fighting at the Club for four years. In his early twenties he had been a runner-up for the Golden Gloves in the light-heavyweight division. He had then, unsuccessfully, attempted a career as a pro. For some reason he had not been able to gain sufficient weight to put him into the heavyweight division for over a year. By the time he had put on the necessary pounds and had accomodated to his new size his interest in prizefighting started to wane. He spent one year as a professional wrestler and then had become a cop. Through some people he knew when he had been a professional fighter he was approached by the Club. He had liked the idea and retired from the Force. Now he was ready to retire from the Club. He had had enough of all this work. His body simply did not respond as well as it once had. He hated getting up every morning knowing that he would have to spend the day working his tired muscles. He didn't enjoy fighting anymore, it was starting to scare him. He wanted to relax with the very satisfactory sum of money that he had accumulated over the four years and enjoy it while he was still able to. He wanted to get fat.

Alex had requested a hearing before the Selection Committee about a week before to discuss his feelings with them. It was his ambition to retire and become a lifetime honorary member of the Club. He wanted to get out while the getting was still good.

"You know, Alex," said Peter Berlin, chairman of the committee, "I must tell you that we are all slightly amazed at your request."

Alex shrugged. He wasn't crazy about Berlin. Never had been. He was one of the Club's real snobs and worked very hard at emphasizing the social gap between the fighters and the members. He had inherited all of his money, which was considerable, and had never worked a day in his life.

"Well, you know, Mr. Berlin, I ain't as young as I used to be. The muscles don't want to do what I tell 'em to anymore."

"I'm surprised, Alex," said Berlin. He always sounded like he was talking to a child when he spoke to a fighter. "We genuinely expected many more years of wonderful matches from you."

"Well, sir," said Alex, "so did I."

"Have you been to see our Dr. Willis yet?"

"Yeah, I have. He said that he had no objections to my getting out. It's not like I'm dying or nothing, I just think it's time."

"Um-hmm," mumbled Berlin as he officiously put pen to paper. He made some marks on the document in front of him and turned it over. Jesus, thought Alex, what a pain in the neck.

"Not only that," added Alex, "but after four years here I been lucky enough not to ever kill nobody and I kinda lost my temperament for that, too. I'd just as soon get out before something happens. I fought a lot of fights here, Mr. Berlin."

"I know that, Alex..."

They asked Alex to please wait outside while they discussed his case and he sat quietly in the hall until they called him back. One of the committee members opened the door and asked him in. It had taken only two or three minutes.

"Alex," began Berlin, "we are well aware that you are one of our senior fighters at the Club. You have served us very well. And, I might add, we are not unfavorably disposed towards your request. Unfortunately, the abruptness of this change would leave us rather short. We do have to find a replacement for you, you know."

"That shouldn't be too hard."

"Perhaps not. But, why, we were wondering, is it that you couldn't wait for the normal time of the year for fighter reviews?"

"Because," said Alex, "now's the time. I know my body best."

"Of course, of course, Alex," said Berlin. "You've just taken us by surprise, that's all." He turned his paper over again and studied it for a second. "Alex... let me ask you this. Would you be opposed to one more match during the period in which we conduct a search for a suitable replacement?"

Alex had pretty much expected that. They always did it. "No, Mr. Berlin, I wouldn't be."

"We'll schedule something not too demanding," he said.

"That'll be fine."
"Well then," said Berlin standing, "I believe congrat-ulations are in order." He held out his hand. Alex was stunned. He shook it.

It had been two days at this point that Mark had been home working on his new slant on the club story. So far he had about five pages. He was tentatively calling it "I Dined At The World's Most Private Club", and, if he did say so himself, it was cute. Harmless but cute. So, no Pulitzer this year, but he was sure that one of the more "sophisticated" magazines would love it. It had been about ten minutes since Linda had called and asked if he would mind if she dropped by. She was in the neighborhood. He pulled on a pair of pants and ran around the apartment picking up his dirty laundry and leftover food. Linda rarely liked his place and there was no point in antagonizing her. He was glad of the opportunity to try the first few pages of his article out on her. Nina had left only about three hours earlier and Mark wasn't at all sure he was up to another demon-stration of his legendary sexual prowess, but, we all must serve as best we can. What a stud he was. Also, he realized later, what a jerk. It never even occurred to him to ask what she was doing in SoHo in the middle of a working day. Linda's office was on fifty-eighth street.

She hadn't been in the apartment two seconds when she blurted out, "Mark, I don't even know why I'm telling you this other than to satisfy my own mind... but, I know what's going on."

Mark smiled. He couldn't think of any other reaction. He was that surprised.

"Whattaya mean?" he asked.

"Look," said Linda, "we don't have to be cute. I know what's going on. I know you've been seeing another woman."

Mark's mind was racing a mile a minute. It was impossible. She couldn't possibly know. There simply wasn't any way that she could have found out. He smiled again.

"Call it woman's intuition if you want to, but there's no point in denying it," she said.

Ah-ha! thought Mark, she's just guessing. She doesn't really know a thing. He got ready to speak.

"I haven't been eating," said Linda, "I haven't really slept in four days and I'm constantly on the verge of puking. It hasn't been a pleasant period for me and I just wanted to get it off my chest."

"Well," said Mark as nonchalantly as possible, "the truth is you don't really *know* that I'm seeing somebody else. You just suspect it."

"No, I know it."

Mark already had his course of action planned. He knew, in the face of what she was confronting him with, that it wouldn't be all that difficult to convince her that what she suspected was really all in her imagination. He could have everything back to normal in ten minutes. He knew that despite Linda's feeling that she was listening to her sixth sense, she was actually reacting to the conversation that they had had a week before. He had told her that although they had been together for two and a half years he still did not want to feel that their relationship was a 100% totally binding one. It was for that reason that he had never asked her to live with him. She said that she understood, because it was the same for her. He told her it wasn't that he wanted to see somebody else, but simply at this stage of the game he needed to feel that if he decided to, he would be free to. In other words, he was telling her what was going on without telling her. She had subconsciously taken it that one step further. So she had suspicions, that was all.

"What makes you think that?" he asked. "I mean what actual proof..." all at once he felt a sinking sensation in his soul. He didn't want to do this. It would just get bigger and bigger and the pain that Linda was obviously feeling would just get greater. "Yes," he heard himself saying, "I am seeing somebody else." He couldn't believe he had just said that. It was alien to everything he had ever done in a relationship before. A friend of his had once given him a rule to live his life by and he had, throughout his adult years, followed it religiously. It was: Even if she finds you in bed with the other woman... deny it! He had just broken that cardinal rule, and he felt great for having done it. It was as if that proverbial stone had just been taken off his neck. He started to laugh. Now, if he could just control that everything would be okay. Linda laughed too. He really couldn't see what was so funny, but they both laughed anyway.

Linda stood up. "Well, that was all I wanted to say. I have to go back to work now. I'll speak to you later."

"Okay," said Mark, "I'll speak to you later." He let her out the door and went back to the couch. He wasn't sure, but he thought he must be dumbfounded.

John Shasky was a strange guy. He was sure of it. Here he was a homosexual... but, he'd never wanted to be one. He had always loved women. Perhaps it was because he had loved them so much that he had left them. All during college he had had affair after affair. Always they had been wrenching, emotional relationships that invariably left him weak and sick. Never once had he been able to establish an easy-going, sexually and intellectually fulfilling relationship. He dreamed about partnerships like that, but they never seemed to come. There was always that inevitable demand and the next thing you knew, the bickering started. Then the fights, then the pain.

It was when he moved to California after having broken up with Sharon Nowack that he first began to feel resentment towards the women he had known. He had a friend with whom he used to go to the gay bars. For fun. They were lively places and the music was always great. He enjoyed the feeling of power that he got knowing that all of these guys craved him and didn't stand a chance. He felt like the beautiful blonde cheerleader in High School that all the guys wanted but never got. Finally, the appeal of loose, casual, easily available sex began to get to him. He found that the idea of one night stands and friendly sex without the hassles that went along with heterosexual relationships just might be the answer he was looking for. He didn't have to worry about telling his life story or impressing anyone or showing off his car. All he had to do was walk in the door, catch somebody's eye and the odds were pretty good that he was on his way home. He came out.

By the time he had met the first man he felt a love attachment for he had already been gay for six months and had had quite a few homosexual lovers. He enjoyed it and had become pretty committed to it. The next thing he knew, the second that love became an element in his liasons, it was the same old story again. First the demands, then the bickering, then the fights and then the breakups. He couldn't believe it. He had effectively become gay to avoid all the discomforts that he had found in heterosexual relationships only to find that it was the same with homosexuals. That irked him tremendously. He felt cheated.

Sometimes he thought about children. He liked children and had always planned on having them. He hadn't thought about that when he'd become gay. It had never really occurred to him that he would become exclusively gay. If anything he figured he would become bisexual... and that only for awhile. And now he couldn't see much hope for any of these things happening. He was still in love with Bill Thomas. He hadn't seen him in weeks and he still couldn't get him off his mind. He had never, in all the time he had been heterosexual, felt the kind of emotions towards a woman that he felt towards Bill. His mother would die if she knew. The worst part was that even though he was resigned to his sexual preferences he was still embarrassed by them. He didn't like for people outside the homosexual community to know that he was gay. He found it very difficult to come to grips with the fact that he was unable to tell his parents. They thought that he had a girlfriend.

Although he had promised himself that he wouldn't, he found it impossible not to call Chicago information and ask if they had a listing for Bill. There were a dozen or so William Thomases listed and about four or five W. Thomases. He called them all. None had been Bill. He knew it was a dead-end at Bill's gym, and he had no idea what else he could do. He saw at least five men a day on the street that he thought, at first, were Bill. The mortifying part was that Bill so obviously didn't want him. He felt like some mongrel dog that had developed an attachment for someone who didn't even like him. Everytime the man threw the dog out he would come back with his tail between his legs. Even if the man drove him to another state and left him there he would still manage to find his way back. He swore he didn't know who had come up with the term "gay". It really wasn't half as much fun as advertised.

Lou Geller had been very pleased with the progress
that Cornelius had made since he had begun training
with Bill. They worked very smoothly together as a
team. Cornelius's progress, in fact, had been so rapid
that Lou was even thinking of scheduling his first fight
with weapons. He had no doubt that he was just about
ready. It was a Wednesday afternoon and Lou had
asked Bill and Cornelius to give an exhibition match in
the gymnasium. Lou did this fairly often. He considered
it to be an excellent training tool for the fighters. It was
a good workout for the men involved, good instruction
for the men who watched and served to generate a little
midday excitement. Matches like this were always announced on the bulletin board a couple of days in
advance and usually drew five or six members who
would come over from their offices to watch.

Bill and Cornelius were fighting with long wooden
staffs. They were wearing more padding than they
would if it had been a genuine fight. They had on hel-
mets and chest, back, knee and elbow pads. When the
bell rang they approached each other very quickly in
the center of the mats. The men, who were gathered
around them in a fairly tight circle, shouted loudly,
egging them on. It was easy to see that the two fighters
had worked together long hours. They both knew each
others moves very well. When Cornelius swung, Bill
would parry and when Bill would take a shot at Cornelius he, too, would block it effectively. Bill was not
losing the opportunity to fine tune Cornelius's technique as the fight progressed. He encouraged the young

119

fighter and chastised him when certain moves that he made were incorrect. On more than one occasion Bill broke through Cornelius's defense and sent him sprawling with a blow to the back or side. Cornelius would only redouble his efforts and come back at Bill twice as hard.

"Hey, cool down, Tarzan," said Bill. "I told you a hundred times to relax!"

Cornelius swung at Bill's head. Bill blocked the blow and hit Cornelius on the ass. Cornelius swung around and tried to connect with Bill's head again.

"Calm down," said Bill as they passed close to each other. "You gotta fight with your head. Otherwise you miss all the good stuff that can happen." Bill caught Cornelius's staff over his head with his own. He stepped behind him and, using the leverage of their staffs, turned Cornelius over his leg. He fell to the ground.

Cornelius was sweating and breathing hard. He was getting madder and madder. He wanted to smash Bill's head for him. In training it was one thing, but in front of all these men he was making him look like a fool. Cornelius got back slowly to his feet and started to come after Bill again.

"Hey, Cornelius, you're forgetting everything I told you."

He swung wildly at Bill again. Lou was a little disappointed. He hadn't expected that Cornelius would get so hot under the collar. That wasn't good.

Bill feinted at Cornelius's head and when he ducked and raised his staff to block, Bill thrust his own staff between Cornelius's legs and tripped him. Some of the men laughed. Bill reached forward to help Cornelius up. As he got closer to him Cornelius spit in his face and swung his staff low to the ground. It caught Bill across the ankles and caused him to recoil in pain.

Cornelius jumped to his feet and hit Bill across the head as hard as he could. As Bill fell to the mat Cornelius rammed him in the throat with the end of his staff. Two of the other fighters ran across the mat and grabbed Cornelius from behind. He strained against them and tried to fight them, too.

"Call Dr. Willis and get him over here right away," yelled Lou as he got to Bill's side. He could see he was having difficulty breathing. He rasped loudly as he tried to get air into his lungs. There was blood around his mouth. Lou and Jeff Simpson picked him up and carried him through to one of the cots in the locker room.

"Lou," said Simpson, "I think he got his windpipe broke."

"Yeah," said Lou, "I think so, too. Did anybody get that doctor on the phone," he shouted.

"Yeah," said one of the men, "he's on his way. He said to try and keep his as quiet as possible."

Bill Thomas, 35, died before the doctor arrived.

The fighters milling around the gymnasium were, for the most part, very silent. None of them knew quite how to react. Nobody had ever died in an exhibition match before. It was unheard of. Cornelius Francis was the most confused of all. He couldn't comprehend his emotions. On the one hand he felt totally lost. He had not wanted to kill Bill Thomas, although he had certainly wanted to hurt him. He had embarrassed him terribly. On the other hand he felt an incredible swelling of pride. He had killed Bill Thomas, the most famous fighter of them all. He had taken him by surprise and killed him. Wasn't it Bill Thomas himself who had told him that they all knew the risks that were involved? Wasn't it Bill Thomas who had told him that he should not feel badly if someone should die at his hands, because in reality fighters died at their own hands. They were, each one of them, responsible for their own lives. He had liked Bill Thomas very much. But now he, Cornelius Francis, was a real fighter.

Lou came quietly out of the locker room. He didn't know what to do or say. Bill had been his friend. The worst part was he had only been trying to help the boy. What a price to pay. No fighter in his right mind would ever help another fighter up in the middle of a match. Hell, after all, it was only a stinking exhibition. They weren't even fighting with real weapons. It was a lucky shot. Never should have happened. A vicious blow, too, thought Lou. Aiming for a man's throat in an exhibition match. Lou didn't know what to say to Cornelius as he walked slowly to his side.

"Mr. Geller," said Cornelius, "I'm sorry for what happened." He held his head down to show he was truly upset. He was also trying to hide the slightly elated look he knew was on his face.

"Never should have happened," said Lou.

"I'm sorry."

Lou shook his head. He didn't know what to say. This boy had a real killer instinct, but he wasn't ready to fight with professionals. Too hot headed. If Bill had been fighting him in earnest it would be one very dead Jamaican boy on that cot right now. He had half a mind to schedule Cornelius into a match right away. Serve him right. He had misjudged him drastically.

"Listen, Cornelius, you better get on home. I don't think that some of the men are going to be feeling too friendly towards you."

"It wasn't my fault," said Cornelius defensively.

"You're wrong... it was your fault. This was an exhibition, not a match. You had no right to hit Bill in the throat like that."

"But I had to. He would have done it to me. He told me never to be generous."

Simpson came out of the locker room and crossed the mats in the direction of the bar. He made a point of passing right by Lou and Cornelius, bumping sharply into the boy.

"Little shit..." he said under his breath.

"Cornelius," said Lou, "go home. I'll speak with you later."

As Cornelius went into the locker room to gather up his gear, Lou went into his office. He would have to make arrangements for the ambulance that the Club maintained to pick up the body. The ambulance, which looked like a beat up old van but carried the latest equipment, would pick Bill up at around 4 o'clock in the morning and take him to the Club's house off Connecticut. There was a small crematorium there. Bill's remains would be disposed of before dawn.

Peter Berlin was 45 years old. He was not married and never had been. He kept an apartment in New York, a beautiful duplex, but the majority of his time was spent at his parents' polite little forty-four room house on Long Island. He had no occupation, as one was not needed. Neither did his father. Nor his father before him. They were gentlemen of leisure. They were of that rare breed that truly believes it is their right to live apart from the rest of the world. A God given reward for their superiority. The vast amounts that he spent, however, qualified him as a professional consumer. This was his place in society. He was a conduit for funds, personally spending enough each year to keep two hundred families employed. He liked to be called a "socialite".

He wore a toupee to enhance his youthful image. He had had a nose job when he was thirty and he had had his chin tailored slightly when he was thirty-two. Most people found it rather hard to believe, but he actually called his mother "Mum". Nobody had ever seen him with a woman or a man, and it was generally believed that he was asexual. He was affiliated with all the most exclusive organizations in town, but the most prized of these was his membership in the Club. He regarded the fighters there in much the same way that he did the thoroughbreds he kept in his stables. He took great pride in their appearance and well-being and charted and analyzed their performances regularly. Bill Thomas had been his favorite. It was with a deep sense of personal loss that he received the news of his death. He would be a very hard man to replace. And, in his position as Chairman of the Selection Committee he was well aware that this only served to increase the problem presented by Alex Nogrady's impending retirement. He was very displeased with the entire situation, and it was with reluctance that he anticipated beginning the search for replacements.

"Quite frankly, Henry," he had said to Ostling, "I really don't know how I'm expected to find two suitable recruits on such short notice. Our files are unusually low right now."

"Now, now, Peter, I'm sure that you'll be able to find exactly what we need. You always do."

Berlin snorted. "That's all well and good for you to say... you're not the one who has to do the looking."

"Would you like me to?" asked Henry sharply.

Berlin was shocked. He was only exercising his privilege to complain a bit... hardly looking to vacate his position. He sighed loudly. "Well, I suppose I'll just have to get to it then," he said. "God alone knows where I'm going to find two qualified candidates, though."

Ostling only smiled. He loved talking with Berlin. It

made him feel so accomplished.

Ever since they had started seeing each other, Nina had tried to convince Mark that everything should be brought out into the open. Not wise, Mark had said. He told her that as far as he was concerned, the only thing they could hope to accomplish by a move like that would be to force themselves into each others arms on the rebound. They would effectively be eliminating any chance of having something real develop between them. She could see that, couldn't she? Eventually she had to agree with him. It did make sense. By letting their passions run away with them, he had said, they could only succeed in hurting themselves and their lovers. What a line! The only reason Mark was really trying to keep everything secret was because he, spoiled brat that he was, wanted to have his cake and eat it too. He wasn't able to reject Linda in favor of Nina because he hadn't made up his mind how he felt about her yet, and he also wasn't able to reject Nina in favor of Linda, because he hadn't made up his mind about her either. This, he was well aware, was a little hard to believe, given the fact that he and Linda had been together at this point for over two years. But, nevertheless, it was the case. Mark's problem was that in relationships he was always looking for perfection. He really believed that somewhere in this world there existed that perfect woman that he had dreamed about all his life. It was

hard for him to understand what was so terribly difficult about finding a girl to satisfy his relatively modest
demands. Rich, beautiful, intelligent and an endless
source of pleasure to be with. Big deal, he thought,
other people had asked for and gotten much more than
that.

It was the little things that bugged him. A mole here,
an extraneous hair there. And, if it took him years to
get over things as small as that, how long would it take
him to get used to the entire person? He was crazy
about Linda and he was crazy about Nina, but perhaps
he wasn't crazy enough about either one of them. Well,
it no longer mattered anyway, as Linda had made the
decision for him. He called Nina and, stretching the
truth just a drop, told her the news. He had finally
decided that it would be best for all concerned if things
were out in the open, so he had told Linda that he was
seeing another woman. Using the old guilt technique,
he then told Nina that he felt it was about time she did
the same with her boyfriend Steve. She was pretty impressed with Mark's ability to make a decision that she
had finally become very comfortable avoiding and immediately called her boyfriend and let him know what
was going on. Now everybody knew about everybody
else and things could move logically and steadily towards their inevitable tragic conclusion. Mark was
sure, beyond a shadow of a doubt, that the upshot of all
this would be that he would wind up with neither one of
them. As amazing as it seemed to him, he didn't particularly care.

Howard Goldberg

The article he had been working on had begun to develop rapidly as he threw himself that much more strongly into his work. The hell with all this relationship crap had become his attitude and he found, for the first time in his life, that he was really writing. Elements that he had never even thought about before started to become conscious considerations for him. Style, technique, construction. It was phenomonal. This time he knew that he was working on something that was not only excellent but saleable. He was positive he'd have no difficulty selling the finished article to the magazines. What had started out as only an effort to salvage something from all the work he'd put into his "investigative" piece was becoming a wonderful project in its own right. It was mysterious, funny and evocative. It hinted broadly at the truth and yet left enough doubt in the readers' minds to entice. It named no people but developed wonderful characters by description alone. They would wonder if such a place really did exist or if it was just a creation of the writer's imagination. He loved reading it over and over, and was sure that it would be no more than a week or two before he would be able to start taking it around to some of the publishers. Who knew... an idea like this could even get picked up for the movies. Well, anyway, it was infinitely more exciting than the troubles he was having with his women. So, if he was lonely later on he could always drown his sorrow in his soon-to-be, newfound fame.

"You know, Paul," said Katherine Flynn, "I hate to admit it, but I truly do worry about Mark."

"You're hardly alone in that respect," said the Senator. They were getting dressed for a cocktail party they had been invited to that evening. One of the more influential lobbyists for the oil companies was having some people over and the Senator and his wife were always ready for an evening of conversation and food. There was no better forum for his views than a room full of upperclass snobs that disagreed with everything he said. The more they disagreed the more he argued. And, as everyone knew, he loved to argue. Plus, he understood that Les McCormick was supposed to be there and he was looking forward to riding him a bit about that "secret club" Mark had told him about. The Senator loved to tease rich people. Especially rich, important men who, despite their positions in society, still found it necessary to act like little boys. He was planning on giving him a thorough going over.

"I'm so embarrassed these days when people ask me how Mark is," said Katherine, "because I know the inevitable next question is, 'and what *is* he doing?' "

"He's writing," said the Senator as he put a few finishing touches on his hair. He had a thick head of salt and pepper hair. It was a trademark of sorts, and he was very careful with it.

"Oh, Paul, please... I find it terribly difficult to keep repeating that to people. I can just hear them thinking, 'if he's writing, why aren't we reading?' "

"I'm sure most people are well aware how difficult it

is to get published."

"They are not! It's not their concern. And what's more, it's twice as embarrassing inasmuch as he's Senator Flynn's son. How difficult would it be for his father to find some kind of a position for him?"

"Well, my dear, it wouldn't be terribly difficult at all. The problem is that Mark doesn't want a position. He's determined to be a freelance writer. He wants to be able to work on whatever he decides he wants to work on, rather than whatever some editor deigns to assign him. I can understand that."

"Well, I'm afraid I can't," said Katherine. Most of her friends' sons that were Mark's age and *younger* had long since established themselves in careers. Many of them were doctors and lawyers and God knows what else. Some of them were even married with children... but, not Mark. "You know, Paul, the terrible thing is that he has a wonderful head on his shoulders. He just doesn't seem to have any desire to use it."

"I don't know how true that is. He's always working on some kind of an article. In fact he was just telling me all about one he's working on now."

"Well, most of his things that I've read have hardly been earth shattering. Really, Paul, they've only been minor efforts at best."

"I suppose he has to develop his style."

"Develop his style? He's been developing his style for over eight years!" She slipped as she tried to pull her shoe on.

"Why don't you sit down and do that."

She sat down on the edge of the bed. "And what's more, I don't understand why you're defending him when you know perfectly well that you'd just as soon see him doing something else as well."

"Um-hmm." The Senator finished putting on his tie and reached for his brush again. He looked at Katherine in the mirror. He could see her over his shoulder. They certainly made a handsome couple, he thought. It was hard to believe that she was the mother of three grown children. And himself, a grandfather... amazing.

"Well, you know, Katherine, he's inherited that stubbornness we Flynns have always been famous for. This is just the type of thing that Mark is going to have to get out of his system by himself."

"And if he never does?"

"Oh, he will... he will... they always do. I was a bit of a rebel myself when I was his age."

Katherine came over and put her arm around his waist. They looked at each other, standing side by side, in the mirror. "When you were his age, my greying rebel," she said, "you had been married five years, had two children and were working full time as an attorney."

"But," he smiled, "I was fighting against it all the time." They both laughed.

V

"Hey, Les," called the Senator from across the crowded room. "How are you?"

Les McCormick waved back to Paul Flynn. As he did, the Senator did something very strange. McCormick wasn't quite sure what the significance of it was, but he didn't give it much thought. Flynn was known to do many strange things. Instead of waving back at him the Senator had opened his eyes as wide as he could, raised his left hand with the fingers spread high in the air and pulled the lid of one eye down with his other hand. McCormick swore he couldn't understand why he had ever voted for the man.

"Paul, what in the world are you doing?" said Katherine under her breath.

"Just having a little fun."

She shook her head in exasperation. "Do you think we could get a drink?"

"Fine with me," said the Senator. As they worked their way towards the bar they stopped to say hello to half a dozen of their acquaintances. Some, like Flynn, were elected officials, but the majority were executives and chairmen of the boards of various large companies. These men liked to consider themselves the real force in American economics and considered the politicians, other than firmly entrenched ones like Paul Flynn, as nothing more than transient employees.

"So, Paul," said a shortish man in a doubleknit suit

to Flynn's right, "keeping you busy?"

"Oh, I'll say," said the Senator, offering him his hand. Katherine smiled at the man who seemed to be waiting for the Senator to introduce him. It was, to say the least, a pregnant pause. Flynn shook the man's hand heartily and smiled. He hadn't the slightest idea who he was.

"I'm Wilbur Fishkein, Mrs. Flynn," said the man. They shook hands. "I testified before your husband last year on those oil price hikes."

"Of course you did, of course you did," beamed Flynn. "Very informed testimony, too... uh... Wilbur."

They nodded at each other.

"Well, " said the Senator, "if you'll excuse us, I see an old friend over there."

"See you later, Senator... Mrs. Flynn."

"Goodbye, Mr. Fishkein," said Katherine graciously.

Paul, taking Katherine by the arm, steered her to the far side of the room where he could see Les McCormick standing with Julian Welles, the president of Southern-Pacific Oil. He couldn't wait to get over there and stick the pins in. They approached McCormick from his rear and Flynn touched him on the shoulder. When he turned around the Senator made the same gesture as before and smiled knowingly at McCormick.

"Hello, Les," he said, giving him a sly wink.

"Hello, Paul," said McCormick, "what the hell are you doing?"

"Come on, Les," chided the Senator. He winked again. "By the way... Katherine, this is Julian Welles.

Although he won't admit it, this is really his little shindig. He thinks all he has to do is break out the *paté* and we'll let him and his cronies up the price of oil."

"How do you do, Mr. Welles."

"Very well, Mrs. Flynn," said Welles. "It's a pleasure."

Katherine turned towards McCormick. "Hello, Leslie, how are you?"

"Fine, Kate... which is more than I can say for your husband."

Flynn gave him his most innocent and exaggerated "who me?" look.

"And what, may I ask," said Flynn, "is the matter with me?"

"I haven't the foggiest," said McCormick. "I was just wondering what was the matter with your eye."

"Hey, come on Les. You don't have to be embarrassed," said Flynn. Katherine shrugged at McCormick. She was as much in the dark as he was. "Maybe I did it wrong," said Flynn.

"Did what wrong?" asked Welles.

"Just a little something between Les and myself," said the Senator. "Here, Les, tell me if this is it." He raised his hand in the air again and pulled down his eyelid.

"I swear, Paul, I think you're becoming senile! I haven't the slightest idea what you're doing!"

"You mean this isn't it?" said the Senator with a look of disappointed surprise on his face.

"Isn't what," humored McCormick.

"The secret sign!"

"Secret sign? What secret sign?" asked McCormick.

"Now, wait a minute," said Flynn. "Let me get this straight. I had it on good authority that this was the secret sign for that club of yours." McCormick's face registered shock. He started to turn red. "Now, if I'm mistaken I'd better just go back to my source and complain. I don't know how the hell I'm going to get in the door without the secret sign."

McCormick's face had frozen. He didn't know what to say or do. He was like a rabbit caught in a headlight. Afraid to move in any direction lest it be the wrong one. Flynn loved it. He didn't notice as Welles touched McCormick's elbow.

"Hey, come on now, Les, seriously... if I've got it right, the least you can do is tell me so."

"I don't know what you're talking about, Senator," said McCormick in an uncharacteristically flat voice.

"Well," said Katherine, "quite frankly, neither do I."

"Nor I," said Welles quietly.

"Doesn't matter," said Flynn, "Les and I do... eh, Les?" He nudged him in the side and then made the sign all over again. McCormick tried to smile, but the best he could manage was a sickly grin. It wasn't terribly convincing.

"How could he possible know?" said McCormick. "That's what I don't understand."

"I don't know," said Welles shaking his head slowly. "I just don't know."

It was one o'clock in the morning and the two justifiably worried men were back at McCormick's hotel room. The last hours of the cocktail party had been a living hell for them.

"Well," said McCormick, "he didn't seem to know anything about your being a part of it."

"I wouldn't be so sure."

"No, I'm sure of that."

"He could have brought this whole thing up at any time during the evening. Why did he wait until we were together?"

McCormick had no answer for that. "We'd better call Ostling," he said.

"Now?"

"The sooner the better..."

He picked up the telephone and dialed the number he took from his address book. The phone rang three times before a sleepy voice answered it.

"Hello."

"Hello, Lucy?" said McCormick.

"Yes."

"Lucy, this is Les McCormick. I'm sorry to wake you, but it's important that I speak with Henry. Is he there?"

"Hold on a second, Les." He could hear her rustling in the sheets as she tried to put her hand over the phone. He heard her telling Ostling who it was. He could feel the phone being passed across the bed.

Ostling cleared his throat. "Hello..." He cleared his throat again. "Hello, Les?"

"Yes, hello, Henry."

"What's the matter?"

"Henry, can you go to another phone? I have something I have to talk to you about."

"Is that absolutely necessary? It's one o'clock in the morning, Les. Can't this wait till morning?"

"No, it can't."

He heard Ostling explain to his wife that he had to take the call downstairs in the den. There were some papers there that he wanted to consult. He was put on hold. He and Welles waited patiently until Ostling picked up the call again.

"Alright now, Les, what's this all about?"

"Henry, I'm down here in Washington with Julian Welles."

"Um-hmm."

"We've just come from a cocktail party where we've had a rather disquieting encounter."

"Yes?"

"Do you know Senator Flynn?"

"Not personally, no" said Ostling. How he was beginning to hate that name.

"We think he knows all about the Club."

"And, what makes you think that?"

"Nothing short of the fact that he said so!"

"He said he knew about the Club?"

"Well, not in so many words, but he hinted at it as broadly as one could. How can this be, Henry?"

"Well," said Ostling, taking an audibly deep breath for effect, "it's a long story. Flynn's son Mark is a freelance writer. Purely by accident he got wind of the Club and began looking into it."

"But, this is terrible! Why weren't any of us told?"

"I didn't see any need to unnecessarily worry anyone. Fortunately, the entire thing was nipped in the bud. We were able to convince the son that the Club was merely a private place for members only. We told him that it was a secret society and begged him as a gentleman to keep it to himself. He believed us and swore he would."

"He obviously didn't keep his word," said McCormick. "His father definitely knows what's going on."

"Now, Leslie, don't get upset. All that Flynn knows is what his son knows, and that's essentially nothing."

"But, we can't have Flynn walking all around Washington talking about this. Word will spread and people will start wanting to know more about it."

"I know, I know. I'll be able to take care of this in the morning."

"How?"

"Don't worry, I just will."

"How?" repeated McCormick.

"We have something on Flynn," said Ostling.

"What could you possibly have on Flynn?"

"It doesn't matter. Suffice it to say that it will be more than enough to keep him quiet."

"I'm not crazy about all this," said McCormick.

"Do you think I am? Now, let me go back to bed before Lucy starts wondering what's going on."

"Alright... goodnight, Henry."

"Goodnight, Les... tell Welles I said hello... and, don't worry, it'll be alright."

Ever since the exhibition match that had resulted in Bill's death a large change had come over Cornelius. It wasn't so much a change as it was a return to the way he was before joining the Club. When he was fourteen and fifteen years old and still living in Kingston he had been a street fighter. One of the toughest in the area. He had been in more fights than any of his friends and was constantly in and out of trouble. When he was seventeen he had run away from home and come to Brooklyn where he had hooked up with a pseudo-Rastafarian group of other boys from Jamaica. With them he became involved in a number of petty crimes, including robberies and muggings. Through the intervention of a local "do-gooder" social agency he started to become involved in a neighborhood boys' club boxing program. He was eventually kicked out because of his vicious tendencies. He could never keep himself from kicking an opponent. He had even bitten one boy.

By the time he had been in New York a year he'd been arrested twice, but had gotten away from the police both times before they had even gotten him down to the station house. It wasn't until he was recruited for the Club, through one of the fighters who had come into contact with him in Brooklyn, that his

attitudes began to change. At first he was in awe of the
fighters at the Club. He simply had not been able to
understand how something as wonderful as this could
exist. He sat and watched these heroes train for hours
and, for the first time in his life, discipline started to
seem desirable. He, too, trained himself. If this was
how these men had become as good as they were, then
he would have to do what they did. He trained vigor-
ously for six months. He was a different person. He
kept regular hours, moved into the apartment the Club
provided him, and disassociated himself from the gang
that he used to hang around with.

Once, however, he had killed Bill Thomas, the man
who among all the others had been his paragon, his old
attitudes and desires began to reassert themselves. He
wanted his friends to see how he had changed. He
was bigger and stronger than before. He had beautiful
new clothes that he had never had before. He wanted to
show off. He knew it was forbidden by the rules of the
Club, but he didn't care. He didn't see how it could
make any great difference if he just spent one afternoon
visiting in Brooklyn. He wouldn't tell his friends what
he was doing or where he was living, but at least he
could strut a bit. And, if they found out at the Club,
the worst they could do would be to fine him. They
wouldn't get too mad at him. After all, he had killed
Bill Thomas.

People's attitudes towards him at the Club had become nasty. He didn't enjoy it around there as much as
before. All of those men that he had looked up to

before were cold to him now. He knew it was because they were jealous. Because now they had lost the opportunity to kill Thomas themselves. Well, that was too bad. He was the cock of the walk now, and he would do as he pleased. He started missing afternoon workouts and spent the time goofing off with his friends instead. At least they gave him the praise and the glory he felt he deserved.

One of the men in Cornelius's gang was a fellow named Tommy Morgan. Although he wasn't from the West Indies he still wore his hair in the dreadlocks of the Rastafarians. He didn't have the first idea what their religious principals were, but he loved the look. It frightened people. The Rasta men believed in smoking massive quantities of marijuana as part of their ritual. Tommy liked that part, too. He even affected a Jamaican accent. He was Cornelius's closest friend and it was to him that he did most of his bragging.

Tommy was amazed. "You mean to tell me, mon, that they payin' you that kind of money to be fightin' with people at that place?"

"Yes," said Cornelius. He was grinning with pride.

"And I be doin' the same t'ing all this time for free!" said Morgan. He hit Cornelius in the shoulder. "Hey, mon, I want in on this. I be fightin' as good as you."

Cornelius laughed.

"Well, I can, you know!" The truth was he could. He was older than Cornelius and had been fighting on the streets all his life. He was a large, powerful man who, at one time or another, had engaged in every crime there was. On three occasions he had killed for money.

"You're serious?" asked Cornelius.

"You bet your sweet ass I am!"

"You don't care if you get killed?"

"Who gonna kill me, mon? I be the one who be doin' the killing, don't you know," he laughed. "Hey, I take that money and run!"

"Well, then, I speak to the Selection Committee."

"Thas' my boy," said Morgan putting his arm around Cornelius's shoulder. "You speak to that ol' selection committee." Now, here was an idea that really appealed to him.

It had been three days since Leslie McCormick and Julian Welles had spoken to Ostling when Malcolm Anderson flew down to Washington for the day. After taking care of a few business related appointments that he had made as long as he was going to be in the area he stopped by Paul Flynn's office. He gave the secretary his card and waited while she took it into the Senator. Flynn, with his shirt sleeves rolled up and his tie pulled down, came bustling ahead of her into the reception room.

"Malcolm Anderson, you old son of a gun!" said Flynn as he pumped his arm up and down enthusiastically. "What brings you up here?"

"Hello, Paul," said Anderson. "I was in DC on business... brought me within two doors of here so I thought

I'd stop by."

"Well, that's wonderful," said Flynn slapping him on the back. "Come on in to the inner sanctum. Rosanne, no calls," he said over his shoulder to the secretary.

God, thought Malcolm, that girl must think we grew up together. He couldn't believe the reception Flynn was giving him. You'd think they were long lost brothers rather than casual social acquaintances. Well, that was the famous Flynn style. The Senator pulled a big leather arm chair in front of his desk for Malcolm and sat down in his own executive swivel model. Malcolm was a little surprised. He would have expected Flynn's desk to be more cluttered than it was. There was hardly anything on it.

"So, Malcolm, how's the wife?" smiled the Senator.

"Oh, she's fine," said Malcolm, knowing full well why Flynn hadn't asked for her by name. There wasn't a chance that he had ever known it much less remembered it.

"Couldn't make it down with you this time?"

"No, no," said Malcolm, "not much point in that. I'm only down for the day."

"Oh, is that so? What time is your flight?"

"I'm taking the five o'clock shuttle."

"Oh, too bad," said Flynn. "I was going to ask you back to the house for dinner."

Malcolm felt like telling him he could change his flight. It would serve him right.

"Oh, too bad," said Malcolm, "but I really have to get back."

"Too bad," repeated Flynn. "So, how's business, Malcolm?"

"Oh, fine," laughed Malcolm. "But, you don't have to ask that. You keep closer tabs on my records than I do." They both laughed.

"But, you're keeping yourself busy?"

"Oh, sure, sure," said Malcolm. There was a slight lull in the conversation. They smiled at each other across the desk.

"By the way," said Malcolm, "I saw Les McCormick the other night."

The Senator clapped his hands together loudly and laughed. "You saw old Les, huh. Oh boy, did I have some fun with him the other night."

"So I heard."

"Did he tell you about that secret sign?"

"Yes, he did."

"You should have seen the look on that poor old guy's face when I dropped the bombshell about this sacred secret club of his. I thought he'd die."

"I suppose it was your son who told you about the Club."

'Yes," said Flynn. He was still laughing. "He's writing some kind of an article about it."

"No, not any more. We had a long talk with him about it and he agreed not to finish the article."

"Oh no, Malcolm, don't tell me you're a part of this, too!" Malcolm nodded. "I can't believe this. Do you guys wear special outfits over there? I mean, you don't have a special club beanie or anything, do you?"

Malcolm smiled politely. He couldn't believe what a wit Flynn thought he was. Well, one thing was for sure, the things he was saying made it more than obvious he knew nothing of the true nature of the Club. Thank heavens for small blessings.

"Malcolm," said Flynn, "I couldn't get a straight answer out of McCormick... maybe you can tell me. Is this it?" He raised his hand and pulled down his eyelid again and cracked up. He couldn't believe how perfect this was. In the back of his mind he could see himself still riding these stuffed shirts ten years from now. He loved it. Malcolm laughed along with him.

"I guess you've gotten a lot of mileage out of this, huh, Paul."

"No, to tell you the truth I haven't had a chance yet... but, don't worry, I'll get around to it." He made the sign again, laughed a bit more and then, shaking his head, made a concentrated effort to calm himself down. "I'm sorry, Malcolm," he said, "I just can't tell you how funny this is to me."

"Well," said Malcolm, "it isn't quite so funny to us."

Flynn was surprised by the serious note in his voice. "Hey, Malcolm, I hope that you guys aren't taking offense at this. I'm just giving you a little bit of a ribbing, that's all."

"I know that," said Malcolm. "That's exactly what I told the boys the other day. I said that there wasn't any way that as good a friend as Paul Flynn would consciously do anything to destroy our club."

"Well, of course I wouldn't," said Flynn.

"That's why I'm glad that you haven't told anybody about this yet."

"Meaning?"

"I'm sure you don't realize this, Paul, but the most important element in the makeup of this little club of ours is its secrecy. If people we know start to find out about it then we might as well close up. There wouldn't be any reason left for us to stay open."

"Oh, come on, Malcolm, that's a crock," said Flynn. "Who in the world cares about your dumb little fraternity anyway?"

"We do," said Malcolm. "Very much."

"Fine, fine," said Flynn. This was getting a little ridiculous. He didn't need to be lectured to by Anderson. "Do you mean to tell me that you got Mark to give up that article he was working on?"

"Yes, we did."

"Well, he's a hell of a lot less dedicated to his chosen field than I thought he was."

"No, perhaps he was just better able to realize how important this was. Perhaps he was able to see that he could potentially do more damage than good."

"Oh, come on, Malcolm. Do you mean to tell me that it would make any difference at all if anyone were to know about this club of yours. It's about as interesting as paint drying. The only reason you were able to get Mark to let it alone is because he probably realized just how boring an article it would be."

"That may well be, Paul," said Anderson. "Nevertheless, I can tell you that both I and the other members of the Club would be most appreciative if you could keep this to yourself."

"Malcolm, did you come all the way down here to tell me this?"

"No, I didn't. But, that doesn't make it any less important to us." Best not to make too big a thing out of it.

Flynn was ready to end this interview. He had no intention of knuckling under to a bunch of post-pubescent adolescents and their stupid club. He was amazed that grown men didn't have better things to do with their time. "Look, Malcolm, if it'll make you feel any better, I'll make an effort to keep my big mouth shut. Frankly, I think it's childish and I'm a little surprised at a man of your caliber being involved in silly games of this sort."

Malcolm was disappointed in Flynn's reaction. He could see plainly enough that what he had said hadn't impressed him in the least. It would be only by a miracle that Flynn wouldn't wind up telling three or four of his Capital Hill cronies about the Club by nightfall. All Malcolm had done was bring it closer to the front of his mind.

"That's great, Paul," he said. "I'm sure that the other members will be very glad to hear this."

Flynn nodded impatiently. Enough was enough.

"I told them that there was no way that a man of your breeding wouldn't understand the necessity of being discrete."

"I'm as discrete as they come."

"In fact, coincidentally enough, it was while we were

discussing that Sentex affair that the subject of discretion had come up."

Flynn looked up. He didn't see the correlation. The Sentex Affair, as it had come to be known, had been a much publicized controversy during his last term, that had wound up as a huge feather in his cap.

"I told them that for the very same reason that we were able to understand the need for discretion there, you would be able to understand the need for discretion in relation to our club."

"I'm afraid I don't see your point, Anderson."

"Oh, you know, Paul. Those papers."

"Papers?"

"Yes, the ones that your office uncovered against Morrison."

Morrison had been a young up and coming politico from Flynn's home state. For a while it had looked like he might even be being groomed to face Flynn for his seat in a term or two. He was enormously popular until a worker in Flynn's office had discovered terribly incriminating evidence that seemed to indicate that Morrison was involved in some very illegitimate use of public funds. Flynn had pressed the cause loudly and dramatically in the media and, before any charges were filed, Morrison decided to resign from public life. He wanted to go back into the private practice of law, he had said. The case was dropped but it was still considered quite a coup for the Flynn camp.

"What about them?" asked the Senator warily.

"Well, nothing, I was just saying that the same needs

apply in both cases. Obviously the need is great that my friends and I exercise a gentlemanly discretion in relation to that subject, just as the need is great that you exercise a gentlemanly discretion in relation to our problem."

"What in the world are you trying to imply?" asked Flynn testily.

"I'm not trying to imply anything, Paul," said Malcolm. "I'm just trying to point out to you how we are able to look out for your interests even though we have nothing at stake. That's what I told my friends, and that's what I told Joe Woolsey."

"Joe Woolsey..." said the Senator.

"Yes," said Malcolm.

Flynn nodded his head slowly. He seemed to think for only a second and then abruptly stood and held out his hand to Anderson. "Thanks for coming by, Malcolm," he said. "It's always a pleasure to see you."

"Same here, Paul. Take care... hope to see you soon." Malcolm looked at his watch. It was 3:45. Still plenty of time to catch that shuttle.

Mark Flynn knew that every person's life was a miraculous thing. Each event that occured was the logical next step in an unstoppable progression that continued until death. A child who ate a cherry on his third birthday and twenty years later graduated from law school might never have become a lawyer if he hadn't eaten that cherry. All of these events were interrelated. What's more, all of the events in all of the lives of all of the people on Earth were inextricably intertwined with each other in the same way. It was equally conceivable that if that same child had not eaten that cherry, another child on the Asian subcontinent would not have been relegated to a life of poverty and death at an early age. Who knew?

Linda Hoskins and Nina Fischer had virtually nothing in common. They had never met, and chances were good that they never would. They worked in different fields, came from different backgrounds, hung out with different people and thought distinctly different thoughts. One had blonde hair and one had black hair. One was a writer and one was a scientist. One had never graduated college while the other had a PhD. One had been happy as a child, the other sad. How amazing it was then that everything that had gone into the makeup of these two women, all of the unique and separate events of a quarter century that made up their pasts and determined their futures should lead their lives to somehow come into momentary alignment. Just like the phenomonon that sometimes occurs when two people say the same thing, in the same words, at the same time,Linda Hoskins and Nina Fischer had made precisely the same decision at precisely the same moment. At exactly 10:07 Tuesday morning both Nina and Linda reached for the telephone. It was at that instant that their lives again diverged. Linda, who had a telephone with a dial, got a busy signal, because Nina, who had a push button phone, got through first.

"Hi," said Nina.

"Hi," said Mark, "how are you?"

"Fine... I have something I have to tell you though."

"Yeah," said Mark, picking up the vibes.

"It's all over."

"Whattaya mean it's all over?"

"I mean that I think it would be best if we didn't see each other any more."

"Hey," said Mark, "that's ridiculous. Why shouldn't we see each other any more? Everything's going great."

Nina laughed. "Well, I don't think I'd go that far. Look, I really don't want to discuss it. I made up my mind and I plan on sticking to it."

Mark was at a loss. She wasn't giving him anything to work on. He didn't know where to go.

"So long, Mark."

"But, Nina..."

"Bye..." she hung up the phone.

Amazing, thought Flynn. In all his life he never would have thought that Nina could be that flaky. A long time ago a friend of his had confided in him that unknown to the rest of the world the craziest people were scientists. Especially cancer researchers. They were the worst. The phone rang.

"Hi," said Linda.

"Hi," said Mark, "how are you?"

"Fine," she said. "Listen, I've given this a lot of thought and I've decided that it would probably be best if we didn't see each other any more."

"What is this, a conspiracy?"

"What do you mean?"

"No, no," said Mark. "I'm supposed to ask that... what do *you* mean?"

"I'm sorry, Mark," she said, "but I just don't think that things are going to work out for us."

"Hey c'mon, Linda, don't be ridiculous."

"I don't think I am. I'm sorry, but that's it."

"That's it?"

"So long, Mark."

"Just like that?"

"Just like that..." she hung up the phone.

This was getting pathetic, thought Mark as he hung up the phone. He knew the signs well. It was getting to be a regular thing with him these days. He lay down on the couch... dumbfounded again.

Lou Geller lived in the Bronx near the Grand Concourse. He had been born and raised there and still lived in the same apartment that his family had had when he was a child. His mother, who lived with him, was an invalid and he took care of her. Despite the fact that the neighborhood had completely changed and none of the people she had known in the old days lived there any longer, she still insisted on staying. Lou had tried a hundred times to convince her that it was time to move on. Half the buildings in the area were vacant, and the other half were burned out. Sometimes it was the landlord that torched the building to collect the insurance and sometimes it was the tenants who did it out of spite or to get moved into a city owned relief apartment. There were muggings and robberies every day and Lou wanted out. He was a wealthy man by now and he could easily afford to take them any place they might possibly want to go. But no, his mother wouldn't hear about it. She had spent the good years there and she had every intention of spending the bad ones there as well. She had long since decided that she would die in this apartment. If Lou wanted to leave, that was okay. He could do what he liked. She knew he wouldn't go.

Between his mother and the way things were going at the Club, Lou had been very depressed lately. He had worked real hard on trying to shake the feeling, but nothing he did seemed to have any effect. Ever since Bill Thomas had been killed things had just not seemed the same. Nobody at the Club had reacted well to the way that Bill had died. It was the only out-of-combat death they had ever had. After having fought in Europe during the war Lou had stayed on as a drill instructor in the Marines for five years. Even though he had seen dozens of men die, many of them his close buddies, he was still most affected by the memory of one of the kids that had been in his platoon in 1949. After having gone through all the heat of boot camp the kid's parachute hadn't opened the very first time out. It was wrong. If they had been dropping into France and his chute hadn't opened Lou would have said okay. But, not in practice. Not when it didn't count. That's what he couldn't stand. The idea that Bill had died when it didn't even count.

He wasn't the only one that felt that way. Most of the members did too. He'd spoken to a lot of them, and that was the way they all seemed to feel. But, there was nothing that could be done about it. He supposed the feeling would pass, but for the moment it kind of took the edge off things at the Club. It was like there was a haze over the place and he just wasn't enjoying going downtown like he used to. Especially with that Cornelius kid strutting around all the time like some kind of big shot hero. It really pissed him off, but he supposed that would pass, too.

It was at Wednesday morning practice that Alex got the news about his last bout. He had been waiting anxiously all week and was therefore a little surprised at his own reaction. All along he had thought that he was looking forward to this match. It would be his last one at the Club and he had planned on making it a good one. The possibilities that were starting to occur to him now had never once, during the course of his career, entered his mind before. It was a bad sign. The bout had been scheduled for two weeks from then and he was to go up against Lee Robotti. He had fought Lee once before about a year ago and beaten him. Lee was not one of the more skilled fighters at the Club, but he was regular and strong. His defenses were very good. He didn't win often, but it was almost impossible to hurt him. He also rarely hurt anybody else. He was considered a safe match. Alex couldn't have picked it better if he had wanted to. Normally he would have been pleased as punch, but instead he found himself scared.

Like everyone else, the unexpected accident with Bill Thomas and Cornelius Francis had left him shaken. All of these years he had had all the breaks. What if it was this time that something should happen? What if Robotti got lucky for once in his life and connected with a freak shot? Robotti was a much better fighter than Cornelius Francis and Alex was nowhere as good as Bill Thomas. Yet, Francis had killed Thomas. What if Robotti got lucky, too? Most of the time Alex could dismiss thoughts like this from his mind before they had even half run their course. Now, for a combination of reasons, it was all he could think about. When he was a kid his father had taken him skiing all the time. He had always told him that at the end of the day when you're ready to quit you'll always say to yourself, I'll take just one more run. Never take that last run, his father had said, because that's when you're the most tired and anxious. That's the run where you'll hurt yourself. That was how he was feeling about this match with Robotti. It was the last one. The one he shouldn't fight. He was scared he was going to die. He began working out twice as hard as usual. At least, he hoped, he might be able to minimize the risks. But, how can you fight luck? If it weren't for the enormous amount of money at stake Alex would back out of the entire thing. Easier said than done. He also had his reputation to think of. He planned on being around the Club for many years to come. He had even gotten wind that some of the members and fighters were organizing a surprise party for him after the fight. He might be scared to death, but he had no choice. He had to fight.

"Hello," said John. In response he heard a familiar, cracking voice doing its best Rock 'n' Roll falsetto.

"Ah'm just a lonely boy... lonely and blue... Ah'm such a lonely boy... don't know what to do..."

"Hi, Mark."

"Hi, John... I'm just a lonely boy."

"That's too bad, but I don't think you got the words right."

"Does it really matter?" asked Mark in a weary, mournful voice. "When you're lonely, you're lonely. Lyrics won't help."

"You've touched my heart. What seems to be your problem?"

"Believe it or not, they *both* dumped me."

"Both!?" said John. "This is really too good to be true."

"Thank you."

"I can't think of anyone who deserved it more."

"I know, I know," said Mark contritely, "I've been bad... so bad."

"Oh, give me a break, willya," said John. "You're breaking my heart!"

"Well, I should hope so," said Mark indignantly. "After all, I loved those two women. Two hours ago I had a harem and now I'm thinking of going cruising with you."

"Anytime," said John seductively.

"Not literally! I was just trying to illustrate a point."

"Oh, shucks... and here I thought we were finally going to get you out of the closet."

"Hummph."

"Well, anyway, I'm sorry to hear the news."

"So it goes..."

"I told you not to mess around."

"I'll get over it I guess." He put on a good show, but he didn't really know if he would get over it. He was hurting more than he would want John to know.

"What else is happening?" asked John.

"Not much, just working on that article."

"Oh yeah?"

"Yeah, it's coming along great. I think I might even have it sold already. I'll know tomorrow."

"Hey, no kidding! That's great."

"I don't know..." said Flynn sighing as loudly as was possible. "It's not the same without your loved ones around you to share the joy."

"Hey, Flynn..."

"Yeah?"

"Why don't you get a dog or cat or something. Those guys'll love you no matter what you do."

"Um-hmm."

Ostling was very upset. He had been besieged most
of the day by calls about this Senator Flynn thing.
Mostly, he was upset with Les McCormick and Julian
Welles. He couldn't believe that they would have been
so indelicate as to have discussed the matter with other
club members. Bad news travels fast. It was the first
hint of a leak that had filtered down to the members,
and it was causing a minor panic. Some of the members had even discussed the possibility of resigning.
Fortunately, he had been able to calm them down with
the news of Anderson's visit to the Senator. He would
have preferred not having to spread the story though.
The fewer people that knew about proceedings of that
nature the better. It didn't particularly worry him,
however, as Club members had a great deal of practice
at keeping quiet. It was just the infernal nuisance of
having to constantly repeat the story. He hadn't been
able to finish his dinner in peace that evening. Every
two seconds someone else would approach him and he
would find himself telling the entire story again. Between welcome sips of his coffee and a few bites of his
dessert he tried to finish up what must have been the
thirtieth retelling of the story since his appetizer arrived.

"So anyway, Carl, I'm sure you can see there isn't
anything to worry about."

"It would seem that way," said Carl Fossner.

"And I know I don't have to point out to you that word of this arrangement must never leave the Club. If it did it would certainly eliminate the effectiveness of our hold."

"Of course."

"Like a cup of coffee?"

"Oh, no thanks, Henry," said Fossner. "I was just getting ready to leave."

"Okay then," said Ostling, "take care."

"I will. Thanks for your time, Henry."

Ostling nodded.

As Fossner left, Robert Keliman, who had been watching them with interest, waited a few moments to make sure that no one else would approach and then went over to Ostling's table himself.

"Hi, Henry... got a moment?"

"Hello, Robert," said Ostling with relief. "Thank God I don't have to tell you the whole story, too."

"No, you don't," said Keliman. "I've got one for you."

"What's that?"

"You're not going to like this. I've got some bad news."

"What is it this time?" asked Ostling. He was getting so used to bad news at this point that it was becoming second nature.

"I'm afraid it's Flynn again."

"Flynn! Where've you been, Robert?" he laughed. "That's all been taken care of!"

"Not the Senator," said Keliman, "the son."

"The son?" said Ostling impatiently. "I thought that

was all settled."

"So did I."

"Well?"

Keliman lowered his voice. He didn't want any of the other members to see that he was whispering, but he also didn't want them to hear what he was going to say.

"Henry, I had lunch with Mort Finger today. He owns a couple of magazines, including *Metropolitan* ." He looked up at Ostling's face to see what kind of a reaction he'd had so far. Not good. "We were discussing some of the different things that we were working on, and he mentioned in passing that *Metropolitan* had just given Flynn a $2000 advance on an article called 'The World's Most Private Club.' "

"Please tell me you're kidding," said Ostling.

"I'm afraid not, Henry. I didn't push it for fear of his getting suspicious. But, he told me that when it was finished and published it was going to be as controversial as hell and really send some head's rolling."

"Then the article isn't finished yet?" asked Ostling. He sounded exhausted. Each new turn of events left him a little weaker.

"No, Finger said that they had bought the rights to the story over the phone. He hasn't seen anything in writing yet."

"I suppose we're going to have to get Flynn to stop working on that article," said Ostling.

"Yes, I suppose we are."

Tommy Morgan and Cornelius Francis lied like crazy at Tommy's interview in front of the Selection Committee. They figured, and rightfully so, that a record and history like Tommy's would automatically exclude him from consideration. They hadn't realized just how complex and far reaching the Club's resources were, however, and by the time the interview had been arranged the Committee knew virtually everything there was to know about Tommy. He was granted the actual interview only out of deference to the fact that Cornelius had sponsored him, and Peter Berlin had no qualms about letting him know as quickly as possible that there would be no place in the organization for him.

Potential recruits never knew exactly what the nature of the job they were applying for was. They were only told, after careful screening or acceptable sponsorship, that they were being considered for a job that was both extremely dangerous and extremely high paying. If this description appealed to them they were then taken to a small office that was kept on a lower floor of the Northrop Tower for just this purpose. It could be reached only through the main entrance and elevators of the building and had no connection to the Club upstairs. It was here that they were interviewed by the Selection Committee which continued the process step by step at a very careful pace until the candidate was either rejected or considered safe for a genuine offer. They were so careful about their selection process that less than three percent of those who got all the way to the interview were ever rejected. Tommy was to be in that three percent.

"So then what you tryin' to tell me, mon, is that you ain't goin' to give me this job," said Tommy to Berlin.

"I'm afraid so, Mr. Morgan. I'm terribly sorry, but it just doesn't seem as if you would fit in with our organization."

"Then, maybe you better try a little harder," said Tommy.

"I'm sorry, Mr. Morgan, but the decisions that we make are final."

"Then maybe I have to be tellin' everybody jus' what's what up here."

"I don't think I follow you, Mr. Morgan," said Berlin.

"Look, mon, I ain't no fool! I know everything 'bout your fightin' and your killin'! I know everything 'bout your fuckin' job!"

Berlin looked at Cornelius. Cornelius looked at his feet.

"So," said Tommy, "if you want all your secrets to stay secrets then you jus' better think again 'bout what you sayin'."

Berlin was flustered. This had never happened before. He called Ostling. After being apprised of the situation Ostling took Tommy and Cornelius upstairs to the Board Room. He dismissed Cornelius after five minutes and remained inside with Tommy for half an hour. When the two men finally emerged it was with the news that Tommy would be joining them and that they had reached an agreement.

VI

It was about three o'clock in the morning when Tommy
Morgan came out of the subway and started slowly
working his way towards SoHo. He had cased the area
the past three nights and, at this point, pretty much
knew where he might expect to find people at that hour.
Flynn's building was a snap. Tommy was always glad
to see that most people never gave security a second
thought. Flynn had a fire escape that went directly up
to one of his windows. The window had no gate on it
and didn't even have an adequate lock. The panes of
glass looked like they had been put in over forty years
ago. The putty all around their edges was dried and
cracked. He wouldn't even have to break the window.
He could probably just push the glass right out of the
frame. The fire escape let into a completely deserted
alley. It was a perfect setup. He would have no problem.

He had his dreadlocks tucked into a knit cap and
made a point of walking in a hunched over position. He
saw no reason to give people anything to remember.
When he got into Flynn's apartment he would let his
hair out. That way if Flynn gave him any trouble the
hair would probably scare the shit out of him. Morgan
loved this type of work. He had gotten so used to it over
the years that it felt more normal to him than anything
else. When he was a kid he had always gotten involved
to prove that he was tough. Now, he didn't have to
prove a thing. He just had to do it. The first time he had

killed a man he had been fifteen years old. A man had given him $100 to do it, and he had hit another man he had never seen before over the head with a baseball bat. He had felt the man's skull crack and then had run like hell. Now he was twenty-eight years old and Ostling was paying him $100,000 to kill Mark Flynn. He'd never heard of, much less seen, that much money. He wondered if this Flynn knew just how much he was worth. He was sure he'd be proud if he did.

Tommy spent about fifteen minutes in the area of Mark's building checking for signs of life before he went into the alley. He climbed up the fire escape as quickly as he could and then sat for five minutes outside Mark's window. When he finally felt the time was right he put masking tape all over the window pane and gently tapped it with his fist. He could feel that it was going to pop out and exerted a little more force. It gave, and he was able to stop it from crashing into the room. So far he had made almost no noise. As he entered the room he took out a pistol he was carrying. It was an old .22 caliber target pistol that he had bought years ago on the street. He had used it in every job that he had pulled since then. It was his good luck charm. As he pulled off his knit cap and stuck it in his pocket he heard some rustling noises coming from the far end of the room. All at once a light went on and he saw Flynn standing next to the lamp in his underwear.

"What the fuck..." Flynn managed to get out before one of the most terrifying figures he had ever seen in his life started moving towards him at full speed.

"All right now, mon, don't be movin' and you won't get hurt," said Morgan pointing the pistol at Flynn. "Don't get nervous, I don't want to hurt you or nothin'." He pulled Flynn by the arm with incredible force and virtually threw him into the chair. "Now," he said, "I want you to jus' sit there an' be quiet while I have me a look around."

Flynn was no hero. He sat still. Tommy worked his way very quickly around the apartment putting things in his pocket as he went. Some things he knocked on the floor. Tommy went over to the desk. "You keep any money here?" he asked.

"All I've got's what's in my pants pocket over there. It's all yours, man."

"You don't have no safe or nothin'?"

"No," said Flynn. Amazingly cool, he reflected, for someone who was being held at gunpoint. Just do what he says and give him what he wants. He couldn't help thinking he should have probably listened to his father and moved uptown.

Morgan started going through the drawers of the desk. Flynn was surprised to see that he seemed to be looking at the various papers, trying to read what was on them. In the middle drawer he came across the first draft of the club article. He thumbed through it for a few seconds, folded it and then stuck it in his pocket. Flynn began to see the light.

"Aha," he said, "so that's what this is all about." He started to stand, feeling a little more secure now that he knew what he was dealing with.

Morgan wheeled towards Flynn sharply. "I thought I told you not to move!" he yelled. Flynn put his hands out in front of him to show that he meant no harm. Morgan grinned and pulled the trigger. He had intended to kill him with a knife, but this would have to do. Flynn fell, clutching his chest.

Jesus Christ, he could hear himself think, I've really been shot. It burned like hell. He heard Morgan's footsteps on the metal fire escape. Here he was back in the movies again with everything spinning and the world going black all around him. He felt light. So this was it. So this was death. Not so bad. At least now it was out of the way and he wouldn't have to live in fear of it anymore. Would his consciousness disappear? Why wasn't his life passing before his eyes?

Flynn woke up in a hospital bed. It was too classic to believe. He looked around the room. There were flowers everywhere. His side hurt. He pulled back the sheet and saw that his chest was wrapped up. All at once he had a sudden rush and he relived in a second the entire experience. He felt the bullet hit him again. It passed as quickly as it had come. He looked around until he found the buzzer and rang for the nurse. The door to his room opened slowly and a little head in a white cap peered around the edge.

"Hello, Mr. Flynn," said the head. "How do you feel?"

"I'm okay, I guess," said Mark. "Where am I?"

"You're in St. Vincent's."

"St. Vincent's?"

"Hospital," said the nurse.

"I kind of figured..." said Mark indicating the room with his eyes. The nurse giggled. She still had only her head poking in the room.

"Uh... would you like to come in?" asked Mark.

"Oh, I'm sorry, Mr. Flynn," she said. "I have some people here to see you." She opened the door wider and let two visitors pass by. It was his father and John Shasky.

"Hello, son, how are you feeling?"

"I'm okay, I guess. How long have I been here?"

"They brought you in last night," said John. "For once a cop was in the right place at the right time. One was passing by your building in a patrol car, heard the shot and came in."

"Was I hurt bad?"

"No," said the Senator. "You were lucky. The bullet passed right through your body and hardly touched a thing. It missed your heart by two inches."

"So what do you think, Dad? Do I get a purple heart or what?"

"The first thing you get is a new apartment. I've told you a hundred times that it wasn't safe living in that neighborhood."

"It wouldn't have mattered where I was living in this case."

"What do you mean?"

"Well, the guy who did this may have done his best to make it look like just a robbery, but you know what the main thing was he took?"

"No."

"He took my article on that club!"

"Oh, Christ! Not that club again," moaned John.

"I thought you'd given up on that article," said the Senator.

"No way," said Mark. "What made you think that?"

"John," said the Senator turning towards Shasky, "would you do me a favor and wait out in the hall for a minute please." John was surprised. Mark looked at him quizzically and shrugged his shoulders. He left the room and the Senator pulled his chair up closer to the bed.

"Mark," he said, "I think you're starting to jump to conclusions again."

"Jump to conclusions!" yelled Mark. "Dad, these guys tried to kill me last night!"

"Mark, I think you're mistaken. I think that you were robbed last night by some drug addict looking for money. And, that's all."

"What?" said Mark. "A drug addict who needed something to read on the way home so he took my article! Dad, I'm telling you, it was these guys again!"

"Son, I know some of the men who are involved in that club and what you're saying is impossible."

"The hell it is, and I'm the almost living proof of that!"

"I don't agree, but I will say this. I think that you

should simply let all of this drop now. It's become a preoccupation with you. You could develop an ulcer."

"An ulcer! I should live so long... and I'm not kidding. If they've tried once and failed, they'll try again!"

"Son, you're barking up the wrong tree."

"Maybe, maybe not," said Mark. "How long am I supposed to be in here anyway?"

"The doctor said that barring any unforseen eventualities you should be able to go home in two or three days."

"Great! Then in two or three days we can start to find out what the hell is really going on at that place. I'll be damned if I'm going to sit around like some kind of a clay pigeon waiting for them to bump me off!"

"In two or three days," said the Senator, "the only thing that you're going to do is come down to Washington where your family can take care of you."

"In a pig's eye! I was all set to believe the crap those guys fed me up there, but I can see I was just being a jerk. They're hiding something phenomonal that they're willing to kill to protect and if you can't see that then you're as stupid as I was."

"Look, son," said the Senator putting his hand on Mark's arm, "I want you to do me a favor. Let this whole thing drop. You're not helping yourself and things can only get worse."

"What are you talking about!" said Mark. "I'm not letting anything drop!"

"Please, Mark, you're dealing with things that you don't understand."

"What are you saying? Do you know something I don't know... don't tell me you're involved in all this!"

"No, I'm not involved in anything. I just don't want to see you continue to harass these people. I know that you think they have something to do with all this, but I'm sure they don't. Please, Mark, do me a favor and let it drop."

"I'm sorry, Dad, I can't do that."

News of the robbery and shooting of Senator Flynn's son made front page in the New York papers and was picked up by all the wire services. Morgan, never thinking for a second that Flynn would survive the encounter, had made no attempt at disguising himself and the articles were all accompanied by a very accurate composite drawing made by the police from Mark's description. It wasn't until the papers had come out the following morning that he and Ostling had known that Flynn was still alive. Ostling had immediately rounded Tommy up and brought him to the Club. He was sure that things would be much better if Tommy were to stay in one of the guest bedrooms until he had had a chance to decide what to do. For the moment he had no desire for Morgan to be running all around the streets of New York with that $100,000 he'd given him. He had him cut off his dreadlocks. It didn't really have the anticipated effect, though. Tommy still looked frightening as hell.

As the members who had seen him at the Club saw the composite drawing of Morgan and started making the connection between him and Flynn the phone calls started coming in. To everyone that called, Ostling told the same thing. First, not to mention it to anyone else, and second, that there would be a meeting at 6 o'clock that evening to discuss the problem. Could they make it? He was not surprised that they all said they could.

Well, thought Ostling, so much for the famed closed mouths of their club members. Although he had spoken to only twenty people about the meeting there were well over one hundred members crowding the Board Room at five-thirty. By six o'clock, when the meeting was scheduled to start, the number had swelled to one hundred and fifty, and they had to move into a larger room. Ostling did not like the idea of having to address such a large body. And, as if it wasn't going to be difficult enough to justify the action that he had taken on their behalf, that afternoon he had read Flynn's article. It was nothing. There had never been any threat to either the Club or himself. Attempting to take another man's life was bad enough, but in the face of absolutely nothing... He had burned the article and had no intention of ever mentioning its lack of damning evidence to anyone.

"Gentlemen," he began. The room immediately quieted. "Gentlemen, I'm both pleased and disappointed in the turnout I see here. I had hoped that the majority of our members could be spared the aggravation of this situation. That, after all, is what I construe to be one of my major functions as Chairman of this club."

"What exactly is going on, Henry?" asked a voice from the middle of the room.

"For a short while we went through a minor crisis. It appeared that we were in danger of being exposed."

"How long has this been going on?"

"About a month ago we first became aware that this Mark Flynn was attempting to investigate our club. He initially became aware of our existence through a friend of Bill Thomas. Thomas had made a minor slip-up. Flynn then in turn told his father about us. We covered ourselves very well and were able to stop both leaks. Both Flynns believed that we were nothing other than a social club that desired to keep its existence a secret. I'm sure by now that you are all aware of the means that we had to use to ensure Senator Flynn's silence. We had also been under the impression that the younger Flynn's curiosity had been satisfied and that he had dropped his investigation. Last week, however, I found out through Robert Keliman that *Metropolitan Magazine* had bought the rights to the article that it turns out Flynn was still working on. I then arranged to take steps that I felt would end this threat once and for all."

"Henry," asked Julian Welles, "what exactly made you think that you had the right to commit murder in our name?"

"Now, Julian, let's not jump the gun here. That boy's

not dead you know."

"Do you mean to say that it wasn't your intention to kill him?" asked Welles.

"Yes, I do. I had only intended for Morgan to destroy the papers for his article and throw a scare into him. I felt that an attack of this nature would give him pause to think. I hadn't expected Morgan would actually shoot him."

"Now, wait a minute, Henry," said Murray Weissman. "We tried that tactic once before and you saw where it got us. Do you mean to tell me that you could actually have thought that there was any point in trying the same thing again?"

Ostling said nothing. Weissman turned and faced the other men. "Back when we first got wind of this entire thing the Board Members sent some of the men over to throw a scare into Flynn. He not only didn't get the message, he redoubled his efforts."

"Well, Henry," said Welles, "what about it?"

"So sue me for acting stupidly. Somehow I thought that being attacked by somebody as frightening as Morgan in his own apartment would have a more convincing effect. If I was wrong, I'm sorry. But, that's what I thought." Suddenly he took the offensive. "And what's more," he said loudly, "we don't even know yet that my plan hasn't worked. I'd be willing to bet that we've heard the last from Mark Flynn."

"And how about his father?" asked Welles. "What do you suppose is going to be his reaction to all this?"

"I don't think we'll have to worry about the Senator,"

Ostling laughed. "We've got enough over his head to keep him quiet for two lifetimes to come."

"Attempting to kill his son is not the same as blackmail," said Weissman. "I wouldn't be surprised if he was more than willing to risk his career over something like this."

"I think you overestimate the Senator," said Ostling. "Gentlemen, I can assure you that the worst is over. Things can settle back down to normal now. Our problem with the Flynns is over."

"And what about this Tommy Morgan?" asked a member.

"Morgan?" said Ostling. "I've already set up his first match for two weeks from now against Jeff Simpson." He smiled. He knew that all the members understood what he was driving at. Simpson was one of their strongest fighters, and he always went for the kill. No matter how big and strong Morgan might be he was certainly no match for a trained professional fighter who was a veteran of three years of competing at the Club. Morgan wouldn't know what hit him.

"You know, Henry," said Murray Weissman, "I never had much difficulty in the past reconciling what we do here at the Club. If men choose to risk their lives and lose, then that's their responsibility. What's beginning to happen now, though, is a different story altogether. What if that boy had died? That would have been murder."

"He didn't," said Ostling.

There was very little talking as the room emptied. No

one stopped at the bar for a drink or to check for announcements on the bulletin board. None of the men went by their lockers, and there were no suggestions for a game of poker. In ten minutes the Club was empty save for Tommy Morgan who watched TV in his room and wondered how he could have missed such a simple shot.

Well, thought Mark, sometimes adversity turns into good fortune. To coin a phrase, every cloud has its silver lining. He was lying in his bed, in his own apartment and looking at his own kitchen table. And, who should he see sitting there and talking with each other? None other than his own two girls, Nina Fischer and Linda Hoskins. It warmed the cockles of his heart. Now, he finally, after all these years, had a handle on life. He filed the remedy away for future reference. From now on, if he were to find himself in a difficult situation and there didn't seem to be any way out, he was to remember to go out and get himself shot. Worked like a charm. They were both being so attentive to him. It was as if, in the face of this tragedy, all other considerations had become meaningless. They had even started to become friendly with each other and had exchanged phone numbers so that they could keep in touch and schedule their nursing time correctly. He didn't hurt very much, but still made a point of letting out a little moan every now and then for effect.

He didn't want to lose his advantage yet. The next thing you know they'd both be on their way out the door.

"Are you okay?" asked Nina. Linda looked worried.

"Yes," said Mark in a weak voice, "I'm alright. Really I am." They looked at him as if they didn't quite believe what he was saying. They both sighed. Mark did too. More from contentment, however, than pain.

"So, that was *your* ad!" said Nina. "I can't believe it. I loved that ad!"

"Thank you," said Linda, "but, it was just okay."

Mark was looking forward to a very pleasant period of recuperation. Call him a male chauvinist pig if you like, but he couldn't help loving the fact that they were both great cooks. He moaned softly again. They both looked up.

Mark had given it a great deal of thought during the last couple of days and he had already decided what his next move would be. He knew the names of at least five or six of the people connected with this club, and he had decided that he was going to write each one of them a letter. If they were upset before, it was his intention to make them twice as upset now. He was going to make them believe that things were ten times hotter than even they suspected. He was glad, in the face of what he was about to do, that he had allowed his father to hire a private bodyguard for him. Burglars often return to the scene of a crime the Senator had said and Mark had to admit that he felt a good deal more secure knowing that the large man in the nondescript suit that was sitting on the couch reading the *National Enquirer* was on his side. He was crazy about that bulge under his armpit.

"Malcolm?"

"Hello, Paul," said Anderson.

"I suppose you know why I'm calling?" said the Senator.

"Yes."

"Make it good, Malcolm."

"Paul, I'm sorry. What happened was an unfortunate accident. The man that was sent was only supposed to throw a scare into Mark and destroy the article he was working on."

"Malcolm, this isn't good..."

"I know, Paul, but our man said that Mark tried to attack him and he had no choice except to shoot."

"That's not true," said the Senator.

"Well, that's what he told us."

"Why did you have to send anybody at all?"

"Mark had told us that he would stop writing that article. When we found out that he hadn't some of the people here got a little excited."

"Who?"

"I can't tell you that," said Anderson.

"Malcolm, what's going on over there? What in hell's name could be worth risking my son's life over?"

"Nothing, Paul. Nothing is worth risking your son's life over. It was an accident and I'm sorry. Nothing like this will ever happen again."

"How can I be sure of that?"

"You have my word," said Malcolm.

"The word of a man who's blackmailing me?"

There was a long pause before Malcolm spoke again. "Paul," he said, "if you were anything other than the kind of man that you are, there would be nothing for us to hold over your head."

Flynn didn't answer.

"Paul," said Malcolm, "I promise you that this was just a case of an impetuous decision which resulted in an unfortunate accident. That's all. I give you my word nothing like this will ever happen again. I swear it."

"Mark came very near being killed."

"It's over. Don't worry."

"Alright, Malcolm, I'll take your word. But, I'm also going to hold you responsible if anything happens to my boy."

"Don't worry. Please. I promise you nothing will ever happen to him again."

There was about a week to go until his fight. Alex Nogrady had caught Lee Robotti after their workout that day and had asked him to join him on the outside for a drink. It was against Lee's better judgement, but he figured it couldn't do any harm. He preferred not to have anything to do with an opponent before a fight, but, what the hell, he'd known Alex for years. Alex walked him over to one of the bars on Seventh Avenue. They took a booth in a quiet area.

"I guess you know this is gonna be my last fight," said Alex.

"Yeah, I know all about it," said Lee. "Congratulations, man."

"Thanks."

"You got any plans or anything?"

"Nah," said Alex, "I'm just gonna play it by ear, y'know. I mean I'm gonna stay at the Club and all, I just don't know what else I'm gonna do."

Lee shook his head. "Yeah," he said, "that's great. Boy, I sure wish I could say it was gonna be me."

"Hey, soon enough," said Alex. He raised his glass. Lee touched it with his own.

"Salut," said Lee.

"Salut," said Alex. He took a drink from his glass and put it down. He was a little uncomfortable and didn't know how to say what he had on his mind. "Listen, Lee, I got something I wanna discuss with you."

"Shoot."

"Well, it's like this. You know, ever since all that stuff that happened with Bill Thomas I've been a little worried."

"Yeah," said Lee.

"Yeah. You know I've been fightin' at the Club now for a lotta years, and like I told Berlin I been real lucky so far. I ain't never killed nobody and I ain't never really got hurt."

"Yeah."

"And, to tell the truth, I don't want nothin' to happen now. Not when I'm so close to ending it all. You know what I mean?"

"Hey," said Lee, "I don't blame you, man. I mean you're really right down to the wire, huh."

"Yeah," said Alex, "that's right. I'm right down to the wire."

"So what's this got to do with me?" asked Robotti. Alex had figured the answer was kind of obvious.

"I want you to take a dive."

"Take a dive! Hey, Alex, what're you kidding me?" He looked at Nogrady's face. He thought he could see a small grin. "Hey, c'mon Alex," he reached across the table and poked him in the arm. "Who're you kidding? You had me going there for a minute." He laughed.

"I ain't kidding, Lee. I don't want to take the chance on hurtin' you and I don't wanna take a chance on gettin' myself hurt. And that's it. I'm dead serious."

"Did you ever do this before?" asked Lee. He'd never even heard of such things happening at the Club.

"No," said Alex, "I never did it before. I never even thought of it. But, this time it's different."

"Yeah," said Lee, "I can see that." He let an ice cube drop into his mouth and bit into it with a loud crunch. He loved to chew ice cubes. "So lemme ask you something, Alex. How come *you* don't take this dive?"

"Because I'm gonna give you a lotta money. I want this last fight to be a winner for me. I'm gonna be around that place for a long time and I wanna win my last fight."

"How much money are we talking about?" asked Lee.

"The whole thing. A quarter of a million."

"Uh huh. And what're you gonna get out of this?"

"For the fight, nothin'. I got a check comin' in for my retirement and I've got plenty stashed away. I don't want a cent for it. You get it all."

"Yeah, well I gotta tell you, I don't know. I never thought about doing anything like this before."

"Hey, think about it Lee. No rush. But, listen, here's a chance to pick up a half million bucks with no risk of getting hurt or nothin'. Don't forget there's always the chance that you could get killed too."

Lee shook his head. He knew that. "Well, listen Alex, I gotta go. I'll think about it and let you know, okay?"

"Yeah, that's okay."

Lee started to get up. Alex grabbed him by the wrist. "Don't forget, this is between you and me."

"Don't worry, Alex. Even if I decide not to do it I still understand why you want to. You don't have to worry about me."

"Okay," said Alex.

"Okay," said Lee. "See you later."

"Yeah," said Alex, "see you later."

Every once in awhile, as he sat at his typewriter framing his letters, Mark would take a look out of the corner of his eye at Mitch Fleischer, his bodyguard. He was stunned that he could actually have been reading the same paper for over two days. Mark would love to have gotten into his head. Mitch had been on the police force from his early twenties until he was forty. Then he had become a private investigator. He didn't really investigate anything, but was usually only hired for his substantial bulk. He had a most impressive presence. When he had been twenty-eight years old a friend of his had approached him with a proposition. It was possible, he was told, that there was a job he might be able to get that carried with it a high degree of risk but paid enormous amounts of money. He liked the idea and was taken for an interview, but was subsequently turned down. The people there had not felt that he was aggressive or intelligent enough. He had stayed in uniform and on the beat for the next twelve years. It didn't much matter, anyway, because it had always sounded too good to be true.

All of a sudden Mark clapped his hands loudly together. Mitch didn't budge. Flynn had just had a brainstorm. All of this time he had been trying to figure out a way of writing a letter that would really put the screws to these guys. The problem was that he was having difficulty figuring out a way of implying that he knew more than he did when they had his article to prove that he didn't. Anyone who read that article would know that he was just fishing. He didn't know a thing. So, he'd enlist the aid of another camp. He'd write the letters to their wives. This was what he wrote:

Dear Mrs. ————————— ,

I feel that it is my duty to inform you that your husband is a member of a private club located on the top floor of the Northrop Tower in New York. The club is actively engaged in enormously illegal activities, the nature of which I cannot disclose to you at the moment. For your own safety and peace of mind I suggest that you check this out for yourself. I'm sorry that, for obvious reasons, this letter must be written anonymously.

He picked up the phone and dialed his father's office number in Washington. The secretary, Sarah Neufield, answered.

"Hi, Sarah, it's Mark."

"Well hello, Mark, how are you?" Sarah doted on him. She had been with his father for fifteen years and had watched him grow up.

"Lonely without you," he said, "but other than that, just fine."

"I heard about your accident," she said. "I've been so worried."

"Now Sarah, don't you worry your pretty little head about me. I'm fine."

"Well, thank God for that," she said. "Mark, your father's in a meeting right now, so I..."

"Oh, that's okay, Sarah, because I really called to speak to you."

"I'm flattered," she said. And she was.

"I have a big favor to ask of you."

"Um-hmm?"

"If I give you a list of names of some Fortune 500 big shots do you think you could dig up their home addresses for me?"

"Why?"

"Hey, Sarah... I want to sell them some encyclopedias, that's why. Come on, what's the difference?" He knew he could count on her, because she had done many things of a similar nature for him over the years. She had always wanted to see him succeed in his career.

"Is this for something you're working on?"

"Sure is."

"Alright then, why don't you give me the names and I'll see what I can do."

"Not a word of this to my father, okay?"

"Okay," she said. "What are the names?"

Mark felt like a kid who was about to tie a can to a dog's tail.

"That does it," said Dick Alston. "Alice is really up in arms now!"

"It's amazing," said Malcolm Anderson, "in all my years in business and life I have never encountered such a persistent pest as this Flynn."

"You know," said Ostling, "he still doesn't know a thing. It's not too late for us to..."

"Oh come on, Henry... what are you talking about?" said Malcolm. "As far as I can see he knows a hell of a lot."

"It's not so," said Ostling. "I read his article."

"You have it?" said Weissman.

"I had it," Ostling said. "I destroyed it after I read it."

"For God's sake, why?" asked Alston.

"Quite frankly, I was a little embarrassed. It was really very innocent. It only talked about a secret club and its members, but it never mentioned any names or places."

"Are you serious?" said Weissman. "Do you mean to say that you nearly had that boy killed over something like that?"

"Well, how was I to know? As far as I could see he knew everything and was about to tell the world. I had to do something!"

"Oh, that's wonderful," said Malcolm. "We all thank you for that."

"The point is," said Ostling, "that it's still not too late for us to do something about all this."

"Should we try and kill him again, Henry?" asked Murray. "That would be a great idea!"

Ostling looked away.

"You know that he's not going to stop with these letters," said Alston. "Guaranteed he'll come up with something else."

"But," said Ostling excitedly, "don't you see that it doesn't matter. None of these ploys mean anything. He still doesn't have the slightest idea what's going on up here!"

"Henry," said Murray patiently, "I don't think that you see the point. He may not know anything now, but if he keeps on digging like this, he will. Now it's our wives he has interested. How do we know who's next?"

"We don't," said Ostling.

"Has anybody considered putting pressure on him through his father?" asked Alston.

"It's a possibility," said Malcolm, "but I think, knowing what a crusader he considers himself, that he'd rather see his father's career go down the tubes than give up his 'quest'. Especially now," he said looking at Ostling.

"I'm afraid I agree with Malcolm," said Alston.

"So where does this leave us?" asked Ostling.

"It leaves us," said Malcolm, "with a lot of thinking to do."

The night of his last fight Alex went over to the gym at five o'clock. The fight was scheduled for eight, but he hadn't been able to sit around his place waiting. He figured he could do some warming up and just hang around a bit. Even though he and Lee had finally reached an agreement the day before, he was still feeling nervous. There was never any telling what might happen once you were actually on the mats. What if Robotti lost his temper the way Cornelius did that time? It was possible. There was never any telling.

For the past five days Lou had been watching Alex

and Lee. At first he hadn't understood why they were spending so much time together. Everytime he looked they were talking. They were always meeting after workouts and leaving together. It just wasn't normal for two fighters to be seeing so much of each other before a fight. When he finally figured out what was going on he was surprised that he didn't seem to care. There was a time not so long ago when he would have been all fired up. He would have fined the shit out of the two of them. Wouldn't have let them fight for a year. Somehow he just didn't care now. Anyway, he guessed he understood, this being Alex's last fight and all. He couldn't really blame him. Ah, what the hell. The members would never know anyway. He let it slide.

Alex and Lee had chosen to fight with knives. They had figured between them that the worst that could happen would be one of them would get cut up a bit. Nothing serious though. Nothing half so bad as what they could expect if they had opted for some of the other choices open to them. No, knives would be just fine.

About seven o'clock Lee showed up. He went directly into the locker room and looked for Alex.

"All set?" he said when he finally found him. Alex was lying on one of the cots.

"Hey, Lee, yeah, how you doin'?" he said. "Yeah, I'm all set. How about you?"

"Me? I'm fine. All set to go."

"Listen," said Alex looking around to make sure there was no one within hearing range. "I figure we gotta go both periods, y'know. Make it look good that way."

"That's okay with me," said Lee.

"Now, look... I'm gonna let you cut me in the second period. Nothing heavy, y'know. Just something small on my calf, maybe."

"Yeah."

"Now, whattaya think about me maybe scratchin' you a bit?"

"I guess that'd be okay."

"Any place in particular I should shoot for?"

Lee thought for a second. He was taking quick stock of where he was already scarred. "Uh, how about trying to get me something light on my back. I haven't got much of anything there."

"Okay," said Alex.

"Okay," said Lee. They shook hands.

"I'll see you out there," said Alex. He got off the cot and went to his locker. He was feeling a little better now.

At exactly eight o'clock Lou came into the locker room and told the two men that it was time to start. Alex couldn't help noticing that he had a strange look on his face. It didn't occur to him that Lou might know about what they were up to. As Lee and Alex came through the swinging doors into the auditorium Alex saw why Lou had looked so strange. The room, which usually sat three hundred, had about thirty or forty spectators. Alex looked up at the clock on the wall. He thought maybe it was too early. For a fight like the one that was scheduled for that night the room was usually filled to capacity. Alex couldn't remember a time in the past when it hadn't been. He turned and looked at Lou. Lou only shrugged. He was obviously as surprised as Alex. Ten of the spectators were other fighters.

Alex and Lee went to their respective corners. They removed their robes and waited while Tony Campisi announced the fight.

"Gentlemen," he began, "tonight we are going to witness a match to be fought with long knives. The combatants are, on my left, Lee Robotti... he is six feet one inch tall and weighs two hundred pounds. He has fought nine fights at the Club and has won four, lost four and drawn one." There was light applause. As much as such a small crowd could manage. "On my right, Alex Nogrady. He is six feet two inches tall and weighs 230 pounds. He has fought 19 fights at the Club and has won 13, lost 3 and drawn 3. Tonight will be Alex's last fight at the Club as he is retiring this year. We all wish him luck." Another round of applause. It was pitifully lost in such a large room. Campisi signaled for the two fighters to join him in the middle of the mats.

"Gentlemen," he said, "there are no rules or regulations in this competition, save that we ask you to confine your activities to the matted areas." They both smiled. They'd heard this many times before. "There will be two periods of ten minutes each. In between there will be a rest period of five minutes. Do you understand?" They nodded. "Please shake hands then and prepare yourselves." They shook and returned to their corners.

The bell rang and Alex and Lee came towards each other. As they circled Alex could see, out of the corner of his eye, two of the members in the stands talking to each other. They weren't even watching the fight at all. The two members both took a last look at the fighters on the mats and then got up and left. Alex stopped moving before he and Lee had even touched.

"Hey, Lou," he called, "what the hell is going on here?" The people in the stands were talking loudly with each other. One by one they started to leave.

"C'mon," said Lou, "let's pack it up."

Lee and Alex looked at each other. They both had the same thought.

Mark had pretty much been up and around for the last two days. He couldn't help thinking that he should have stayed in bed. The minute that he had started feeling well enough to get up things had begun changing in the girls' attitudes towards him. Finally Linda had called and said that she and Nina had discussed it thoroughly and had decided that they would all be best off sticking to their original plan. Now that Mark was sufficiently healed they felt it was becoming too emotionally painful to constantly be around. For the second time in two weeks he was being kissed off by both girls. He was past feeling dumbfounded any longer. He was just wondering if Mitch could cook.

"Hey, Mitch," he said, "can you cook?"

"Can I cook?" asked Mitch looking up from his paper. Thank God that at least a new issue had come out.

"Yeah," said Mark, "can you cook?"

"Yeah, sure," said Mitch, "I can cook." He went back to his paper.

"What can you cook?" asked Mark. Trying to make conversation with Mitch was not exactly the easiest thing going.

"What can I cook?" asked Mitch.

"Yeah," said Mark, "what can you cook?"

"I don't know," said Mitch, "I guess I can make a cheese omelette."

"Anything else?" Mark asked. Mitch looked back at his paper and didn't answer. Mark figured that one must have been too tough for him.

Ever since he had sent out the letters Mark had been gleefully imagining the havoc he must have wreaked. Unfortunately though, he had no way to actually see the damage he was sure he had caused. Plus, he was anxious to do more, so he had therefore decided to get out his camera gear and, once again, start staking out the club's headquarters on Sixth Avenue. He wanted to get pictures of more of the people involved and start to send their wives letters too. He was also going to write letters to some of the various newspapers and magazines and get them interested in taking a look as well.

He had tried to explain as much of all this as he could to Mitch Fleischer in an effort to enlist his aid. Surprisingly enough, Mitch had been very enthusiastic. Mark could tell, because he had said "sure." It was about eight o'clock Friday evening when they loaded Mark's equipment into Mitch's car and set off uptown.

Mark Flynn and Mitch Fleischer parked Mitch's '69 Catalina in the municipal parking lot on 54th Street. Mitch carried most of the equipment as they walked towards the Northrop Tower.

"So," said Mitch, "if these guys shot you how come we wanna take their pictures?"

"Because," explained Mark for the fourth time, "I want to try and get something on them, and this is the best way I know how. I'm trying to figure out what's going on up there."

"So, if you wanna know what's goin' on up there, how come we don't go up?"

"Because," began Mark. He was about to explain it to him again when he realized that maybe it wasn't such a bad idea after all. He looked at Mitch. If he'd wanted an army to help him he couldn't have found a much better one than Mitch. They might just go up there and catch these guys in the act.

"For one thing," said Mark, "they've got a guard on duty downstairs."

Mitch patted the bulge under his armpit. "Yeah?" he said.

Another good point, thought Mark. And anyway, what the fuck. These guys had had him beaten up and nearly killed. What difference could a little trespassing make in the face of all that? "Okay," he said, "let's go up." Mitch nodded.

As they rounded the corner and approached the Tower, Mark began to become more and more aware of sirens blaring. He started to have a bad feeling.

"I once went for an interview for a job in that building," said Mitch pointing towards the Tower.

"That's the building we're going to," said Mark. It was surrounded by fire trucks. Mark looked up the side of the building but he wasn't able to detect any smoke. He started to run. Mitch grunted and started to run also. There was a crowd of people being held behind a police line. Even though there was nothing to see, they were always there. There was never anything to see in a skyscraper fire. Mark went up to the line and called to one of the firemen. He didn't answer. Mark squeezed through two of the saw horses and was immediately caught by one of the men.

"Hey, it's alright," said Mark. "Press." He reached in his pocket and took out his wallet. He had a phony press pass that a friend of his had made for him once. It was tough for freelance writers to get credentials.

"Oh, okay," said the fireman, "just do me a favor willya, and keep out of the way."

"Sure thing," said Mark. "Hey, what's going on anyway?"

"Oh, they got some kinda fire up on top of the Tower.

It was real hot for awhile, but we got it under control now. It ain't gonna spread."

"What's that... on the top floor?" asked Mark.

"Yeah, the top two floors."

"Whatta they got, some kinda club up there, or what?"

"Naw," said the fireman, "there's no club up there. It's just a couple of floors of storage and machinery."

"I always thought they had some kinda health club and stuff like that up there."

"Nope," said the fireman. "There wasn't nothing up there but a lot of junk. Big empty space... fire just swept through like a ball of flames, y'know."

"No kidding..."

"Yeah..."

The fireman started picking up some of his equipment that was lying on the ground and Mark raised his camera. He figured if he was supposed to be a reporter covering a fire he should at least make an effort to look the part. The fireman looked pleased.

"Yeah," he said, looking at Mark, "it looks like it mighta been set, too."

"Whattaya mean... arson!"

"Looks like it."

Mark let the camera fall back to his side.

"Were you up there?"

"Yeah, sure."

"And you're positive there wasn't anything up there like some kinda health club or something."

"Hey, how many times do I gotta tell you... there

wasn't nothing up there except four walls and a lotta fire. That's all. Period."

Mark made a face. This whole thing was starting to get ridiculous.

"Okay, well thanks a lot," he said

"Is that all the pictures you're gonna take?"

"Yeah," said Mark. "I already got more than enough."

"Okay, then take it easy."

"Yeah, you too."

"Hey, my name is Jerry Hoffman. In case you wanna quote me or something."

Mark turned and walked back towards the police line where Mitch was waiting for him.

"We don't go up?" asked Mitch.

Mark shook his head and laughed. "No, we don't go up." They started off in the direction of the parking lot.

"Hey, Mitch," said Mark. "Whattaya say to one of them cheese omelettes?"

"Okay," said Mitch.

ABOUT THE AUTHOR

Howard Goldberg graduated from the University of the Arts (BFA, Filmmaking and Painting). He received a Sundance Institute Fellowship, where he developed the feature film "EDEN," which he wrote and directed. "EDEN" was in the Dramatic Competition at the Sundance Film Festival and played extensively all over the world.

He wrote and directed the cult feature film "APPLE PIE" and wrote (book, music, lyrics) and directed the Off-Broadway musical "BUSKERS." He directed one of the first rock videos, Rod Stewart's "SAILING," for Warner Bros. Records and wrote the novel "THE KING OF CLUBS" (Parthenon Press).

His drawings and sculptures are in many private collections. Among his works is "THE JESTER," an eight-foot tall bronze bas-relief on the tower of a landmark building. A fine art book of his drawings (Morgan Press) is in the permanent collections of many libraries.